Praise for RITA® Award-winning author Beth Andrews

"Andrews combines sparkling dialogue with characters that have real depth."

—*RT Book Reviews*

"Readers can always count on Beth Andrews to spin an empathetic tale with a loving happily ever after."

—*Cataromance*

"Beth Andrews is an amazing writer and storyteller. I can't wait to find another of her books to delve into."

—*Noveltalk*

"If you haven't read a book by Beth Andrews let me just say you're missing out! She's an author you must add her to your list."

—*Fresh Fiction*

"I can only recommend *Not Without Her Family* whole-heartedly. It made me smile and cry—a wonderful comfort read and one I will definitely pick up again."

—*All About Romance*

Dear Reader,

I'm fascinated by family dynamics, from the bond formed between a parent and a child, to the relationships between siblings. I love to see how those dynamics shift and change as marriages evolve out of that wonderful honeymoon stage into building a life, making a home and raising children together. How parents act with and react to their children during their many phases of growth. How families cope with milestones—both those small moments that seem to pass in the blink of an eye, to the larger, life-altering ones.

During the writing of this story, I went through one of those milestones. And while this event was, in the grand scheme of things, small and happy, it has changed the very dynamics of my household. My eldest child, my only son, started college six hundred miles away. One phase of our lives is over but a new phase of his life has just begun. And while I may mourn the ending, I'm proud and excited for my son's new adventure.

Matt Sheppard experiences one of those life-altering changes in *The Prodigal Son*—though not by his own design. He's quite happy with his life and has no intention of ever returning to his small hometown of Jewell, Virginia.

We all know what they say about the best of intentions.

Matt may not have planned on returning to Jewell, but by returning home he finds forgiveness, acceptance and, most important, love.

I love to hear from readers. Please visit my website, www.bethandrews.net,
or write to me at P.O. Box 714, Bradford, PA 16701.

Happy reading!

Beth Andrews

The Prodigal Son
Beth Andrews

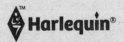
Harlequin®

TORONTO NEW YORK LONDON
AMSTERDAM PARIS SYDNEY HAMBURG
STOCKHOLM ATHENS TOKYO MILAN MADRID
PRAGUE WARSAW BUDAPEST AUCKLAND

Recycling programs
for this product may
not exist in your area.

ISBN-13: 978-0-373-71707-1

THE PRODIGAL SON

Copyright © 2011 by Beth Burgoon

www.eHarlequin.com

Printed in U.S.A.

ABOUT THE AUTHOR

Beth Andrews is a Romance Writers of America RITA® Award winner and Golden Heart winner. She lives in northwestern Pennsylvania with her husband and two teenage daughters. In her free time she visits wineries, drinks wine—both for research purposes, of course—and works on perfecting her recipe for crème brûlée. When not researching (or making fattening desserts) she can be found counting the days until her son returns from college. Learn more about Beth and her books by visiting her website, www.BethAndrews.net.

Books by Beth Andrews

HARLEQUIN SUPERROMANCE
1496—NOT WITHOUT HER FAMILY
1556—A NOT-SO-PERFECT PAST
1591—HIS SECRET AGENDA
1634—DO YOU TAKE THIS COP?
1670—A MARINE FOR CHRISTMAS

Don't miss any of our special offers. Write to us at the following address for information on our newest releases.

Harlequin Reader Service
U.S.: 3010 Walden Ave., P.O. Box 1325, Buffalo, NY 14269
Canadian: P.O. Box 609, Fort Erie, Ont. L2A 5X3

For Trevor.

Acknowledgments

My sincere gratitude to the wonderful women at Casa Larga in Fairport, New York, and Mitzi Batterson of James River Cellars Winery in Glen Allen, Virginia.

PROLOGUE

"WHAT DO YOU MEAN, you've been offered a job?"

Though the words were said quietly, almost conversationally, eighteen-year-old Matt Sheppard knew better than to let his father's mild tone fool him.

He was in trouble.

What else was new?

But at least it would be for the last time. The last time he had to stand before Tom Sheppard, stiff as a soldier in front of a four-star general, waiting for some form of discipline—or worse, one of his dad's long-winded lectures.

Matt forced his shoulders to relax. "I was offered a job at a winery in Napa."

What he left out was that he'd applied for said job. And a dozen others. Anything to get as far away from his hometown of Jewell, Virginia, and, more importantly, the Diamond Dust—his father's beloved winery.

Tom took off his reading glasses and set them aside before slowly leaning back in his chair. His eyes—the same green as Matt's—narrowed on his youngest son. King of his domain, Matt thought snidely. Never did his dad feel more self-important than when he was sitting behind his huge, mahogany desk in his oppressive office with its dark woodwork and leather furniture. Matt's mother, Diane, stood to her husband's right, a hand on his shoulder.

They were, as always, a unit. One entity. Usually against him.

He tried not to fidget even though his dad stared at him as if trying to read his thoughts. They'd arrived home twenty minutes ago from Matt's high-school graduation. And while he'd exchanged his dress clothes for his normal outfit of cargo shorts and a T-shirt, his mom still had on her sleeveless blue dress, her long, blond hair held back in a sparkly clip. His dad's tie was loose, his shirtsleeves rolled up. His suit coat hung over the arm of one of the matching chairs behind Matt.

"You already have a job," his dad finally said, the assumption being that because Matt was a Sheppard, he'd spend his last summer at the Diamond Dust before starting college. That he'd want to stay.

Matt flipped his hair out of his eyes with a jerk of his head. "Yeah, I do." Though he wanted to look anywhere but at his father's stern gaze, he met the old man's eyes. "In Napa. I start in two days."

"Oh, Matthew," his mom said, sounding disappointed. He ground his back teeth together. Besides getting into trouble, he also excelled at disappointing his parents.

Was it any wonder he wanted to escape?

Tom straightened and leaned forward. "You accepted a job almost three thousand miles away without bothering to tell us about it first?"

"I'm eighteen," Matt pointed out, unable to hide the

defensiveness in his tone. "I don't need your permission." He swallowed but the lump in his throat remained. "When Brady was my age, he was already enlisted."

"You're not Brady," Tom snapped.

Matt's hands shook. He slid them into his front pockets. "That's the problem, isn't it? I'm not Brady. Or, better yet, Aidan. Right?"

"That's enough," his mother insisted, her voice shaking. "We don't expect you to be like your brothers and we certainly don't compare you to them, or them to you."

Matt snorted. Maybe she didn't, but he knew what his father thought of him. He didn't measure up. Not to Tom's high expectations and certainly not to either of his older brothers. Brady, a Marine, was serving their country overseas, and Aidan, the eldest Sheppard son was heading to law school. Brady was quiet, reserved and already engaged to his high school sweetheart, the gorgeous Liz Montgomery. Aidan was their father's clone. Overbearing. Uptight. Controlling. He'd make one hell of a lawyer.

"You'll go to California in the fall for school and not a day before," his father said tightly. "In the meantime, you'll work at the Diamond Dust. Discussion over."

Matt balled his hands in his pockets. "I am taking the job and I am leaving tomorrow. But you're right about one thing. This discussion is over. Sir," he added, his tone snide enough to have his father slowly rising from his seat.

Diane laid a hand on her husband's arm. Either in

comfort or in an attempt to restrain him, Matt wasn't sure. "How do you plan on getting to California?" she asked him. "Where will you live? You can't move into the dorms until the end of the summer."

"I'm flying out of Richmond tomorrow at noon. I already have my ticket. Paid for with my own money," he added, before they could accuse him of using their cash for it. "And I'll stay at the winery." He slid a glance at his father. "The owner often takes on workers from the school."

The school being the University of California Davis, which had one of the top viticulture and enology programs in the country. The school he'd busted his hump just to get in to. The school his father had claimed was a waste of time and money since he could teach Matt everything he needed to know about cultivating grapes and the science of making wine.

But that wasn't enough for Matt. He wanted to know more than his dad. Go further.

Be better.

"Now you listen to me, boyo, and you listen good," Tom said in a soft, deadly tone as he laid both hands on his desk and leaned forward. "You'll do as I say or—"

"Or what?" Matt asked, telling himself there was nothing his father could do to intimidate him. Hopefully. "You'll ground me? Take away my truck? Go ahead. But you can't stop me from going."

His dad pushed away from the desk and stalked around it, his mouth a thin, angry line. Matt's chest tightened and he took his hands from his pockets but he held his ground. It still amazed him that, no matter how larger than life his dad had always seemed, he wasn't. In fact, since Matt's final growth spurt last summer, he had a good two inches on his old man.

Too bad he still felt about three feet tall when his dad looked at him the way he did now.

"You really want away from Jewell that badly you can't wait three months?" Tom asked, his hands on his hips.

"I want away from you that badly."

"Matthew!" his mom cried.

But he didn't turn away from his dad's eyes, from the shock and hurt in them. For a moment, Matt debated taking his words back, but he couldn't. Wouldn't. Not when they were the truth.

And then, that hurt changed, turned into icy resolve. "You want to go off and be a big man? Fine. Go. But know this. If you walk out that door, you'll get nothing from us. No money. No tuition. Nothing."

"Wait a minute." Diane hurried around the desk, her eyes wide and distressed. "This is getting out of hand. We all need to take a little time, calm down, then we can discuss—"

"There's nothing to discuss," Tom said, not so much as glancing his wife's way. "It's past time this boy learned what a good thing he's had here all these years. Maybe he'll even grow up a little."

Matt flashed hot then cold. His palms grew damp. All his plans for the future shifted. He'd have to work during school now. Get loans rather than count on his parents' financial support. It wouldn't be easy, that was for certain. But it'd be worth it.

He'd be on his own. Completely.

"I don't need your money," he told his father, proud of how rational, how mature, he sounded. "I don't need you at all."

Tom rocked back on his heels. "We'll see what tune you're singing in a few months when you're paying your own way. You don't realize what you're throwing away. But you will."

"I won't change my mind," he vowed, his hurt and anger giving his conviction the ring of truth. "And I won't be back. Ever."

"Matthew," his mom whispered, "please don't say that, honey. You know there will always be a place for you here. And at the Diamond Dust. This is your home."

He waited. But his father didn't agree with his wife. Didn't say anything at all. Didn't beg him to stay. Or take back his harsh words. He didn't apologize for every time he'd made Matt feel less. Less than perfect. Less than his brothers. For all the times he'd made Matt wonder why his father couldn't treat him like he did Aidan and Brady. Why he couldn't love him the same way.

But his dad didn't say anything. The only sound was that of his mom's soft crying. Matt wanted to go to her, to hug her one last time. To tell her everything would be okay. But he couldn't. He felt too close to tears himself.

Instead, he turned on his heel and brushed past his dad, fully intending never to see his parents, this house, or the Diamond Dust again. When he reached the door, Tom's voice stopped him, his words causing a cold sweat to break out along Matt's neck.

"You'll come back," his dad said, as if he were speaking a prophesy. "And when you do, I'll be waiting."

CHAPTER ONE

He was going home.

Not to stay, Matt assured himself as he steered the four-wheeled ATV down a row between thick, leafy vines in the eastern section of Queen's Valley's vineyards. He shut off the ignition. Never to stay.

The worst part about going back to Jewell? This wouldn't be the first time. No, he'd visited his hometown plenty of times since making his impassioned vow never to return ten years ago. He smiled ruefully. That was the problem with making dramatic, heartfelt declarations. They were hard to stick to. Especially ones made in the heat of anger.

Lesson learned.

Which was why he rarely made promises. They were too hard to keep.

Shaking his hair back, he got off the ATV and unhooked the bungee cords holding his equipment bag to the rack behind the seat. He took out his refractometer and slid it into the front pocket of his loose cargo shorts before grabbing a heavy plastic bag. Going down the row, he picked samplings of the Chardonnay grapes, tossing them into the bag.

Queen's Valley was forty acres of vineyards nestled

along the Murray River in South Australia. The grapes thrived in the warm, temperate climate. All around him the vines reached well above his head with heavy clusters of healthy grapes and a well-maintained canopy, the leaves lush and green. He'd worked at wineries in Napa, France and Italy and could honestly say Queen's Valley was one of the best vineyards he'd seen.

And for the next three years, it was all his.

But first he had to return to where he'd begun. Oh, he'd tried to keep the vow he'd made graduation night. The next day he'd flown out of Virginia and told himself he'd never look back. For over a year he'd kept his distance from his family, the only contact with them an occasional email from one of his brothers, a weekly phone call to his mother. During that time he'd worked two jobs while going to school. Though it'd been a struggle, he'd managed to juggle everything and had put himself through college.

He'd figured out how to take care of himself. And as much as he hated to admit it, his father had been right about one thing. He'd had to grow up. He'd also discovered that he liked being on his own. That he didn't need his family.

Knowing that made it a lot easier to rip up the checks his mother sent like clockwork at the beginning of each month. It also let him swallow his pride and go home for Christmas during his sophomore year. Three days where, for his mother's sake, he'd tried his best to act as if everything was all right. As if all was forgiven.

But during his stay, he remembered his graduation

night. His hurt and anger and resentment that his father couldn't appreciate him for who he was. Couldn't support him in what he wanted for himself.

Then, less than a year after that awkward, tension-filled Christmas, the unthinkable happened. Tom Sheppard, the man who was larger than life, had been diagnosed with pancreatic cancer. Six months later, he was dead.

And he and Matt had never discussed that night or the many issues between them, never came to terms with each other. There were no apologies. No heart-to-heart talks. No closure.

Matt gave his head one sharp shake. That was in the past now. All in the past. He was more interested, more vested in the future. And his future was right here in Queen's Valley. Continuing to pick grapes, he walked down the row, taking samples from different vines and tasting an occasional grape.

For over twenty-five years, Queen's Valley had provided top quality fruit to local wineries. Now the owner, Joan Campbell, had decided to branch out and start making the vineyard's own wines. She'd spared no expense building a state-of-the-art facility and she'd hired Matt to run it all. He had final say in every decision from the variety of grapes to what type of oak barrels to purchase to the shape of the wine bottles. And everyone, save Joan and her daughter, Suzanne, were to report to him.

Total control.

Whistling, he repeated his picking process on the

other side of the row. It was like a dream come true. He got to work for a winery that had everything at its disposal to produce the finest wines. A chance to build on his growing reputation, to be known as the man who put Queen's Valley on the map as one of the finest wineries in Australia.

The best part? It was halfway across the world from Jewell, Virginia.

As he made his way back to where he'd started, he heard the sound of another ATV approaching. A moment later, Joan came into view, her chubby body leaning over the handlebars. Her straw hat, tied around her throat with a string, sailed behind her as she sped down the row at twice the speed Matt would consider safe.

She came closer, and closer still. There was no room for her to get by his ATV without plowing through the trellised vines, but she showed no signs of slowing. Matt's heart thumped heavily in his chest. Instead of running him over, she stopped quickly, her rear wheels sliding. Clumps of grass and dirt shot out from the spinning tires and Matt jumped back to avoid getting sideswiped.

He wiped the back of his free hand over his forehead. Knew the sweat there wasn't just from the heat. "You are hell on wheels," he muttered when Joan shut off the vehicle.

"I'll take that as a compliment."

"Believe me. It wasn't meant as one."

"Now, Matthew, is that any way to speak to your

employer?" Her words were like machine-gun fire—short, choppy bursts that came at a man fast and furiously. Combined with her raspy, smoker's voice and heavy Australian accent, he hadn't understood half of what she said the entire first month he'd worked for her.

And no matter how many times he'd asked her to call him Matt, she still insisted on using his full name.

Joan combed both hands through her windblown gray hair before putting her hat on. She tipped her head up so she could see him from under the wide brim. "I thought you had a plane to catch."

"Not for a few hours." He squeezed the grapes through the bag, crushing them and releasing their juice. "I wanted to check these one last time before I leave."

Chardonnay, along with Pinot Noir, were early ripening grapes. He wanted to make sure they weren't set to ripen while he was gone, since it would be impossible for him to decide they needed harvesting when he was on the other side of the world.

"Suzanne was just asking about you. Why don't you stop by and tell her goodbye?" Joan climbed off the ATV, her shrewd gaze on him. "I'm sure she'd appreciate it."

The nape of his neck tingled. "I'll be sure to do that," he lied.

He ducked his head and pretended dipping the slide of his refractometer into the juice took all of his concentration. At the previous wineries where he'd worked, he'd had to deal with long hours, early frosts, drought, blight…but never a matchmaking boss.

Not that he had anything against the pretty Suzanne. In fact, if the situation was different, he'd have done his best to charm her into his bed. But he preferred to keep his personal life separate from his career. No mixing business with pleasure. No ties. No commitments to hold him to a place other than a legal contract. And when that contract was fulfilled? He was free to go. No hard feelings. No repercussions.

No one trying to guilt him into staying.

Looking through the refractometer, he noted the grapes' sugar content—twenty-four and a half Brix. The higher the Brix in the grapes, the higher the alcohol content in the wine. But the best winemakers didn't go just by the numbers. They took into account everything from the color of the skins and seeds to the taste of the fruit and the health of the vines and leaves.

He picked a plump, green grape and tossed it into his mouth. The sun rose over majestic, copper-colored limestone cliffs. It was the middle of February and he was sweating, his shirt sticking to his back. Even his scalp was burning. The breeze brought with it the scent of the river.

God, he loved it here. For now. And when his time at Queen's Valley was up, he'd be more than ready to move on to the next place. To the next challenge.

"You going to tell me your verdict," Joan groused, "or stand there and eat all of my fruit?"

"Skin's thick," he said, still chewing. "They're fairly

sweet and fruity but still acidic." He swallowed. "They need more time on the vine."

She narrowed her eyes until they practically disappeared in her round face. "You sure you're not just saying that, not delaying our harvest so your plans don't get interrupted?"

He didn't bat an eye at her accusation. He'd quickly learned over the past few months that if he took offense at every brusque, argumentative word Joan said, he'd be pissed off all the time. Besides, he'd had tough bosses before. The most demanding being his father.

And the most important lesson he'd ever learned from Tom Sheppard? Never let them see you sweat.

"You hired me because you wanted someone knowledgeable," he told her, handing her the refractometer and the mashed grapes. "But if you don't believe me, see for yourself."

"Cutting it close," she said after checking the sugar content. "What if they turn while you're gone?"

"They won't. The next few weeks will be cool in the mornings. We have time."

Ripe wine grapes were at their best for only a few days, which made the decision of when to harvest important, but also risky. Matt wasn't worried, though. They'd had a colder than average summer and were experiencing a late harvest year. And the cool, foggy mornings would ensure the grapes finished ripening slowly.

Too bad Joan didn't seem convinced.

"Look," he said, "if they were ready or if there was

the slightest chance at all that they could ripen during the next eight days, I'd stay."

"You'd miss your own brother's wedding?"

Miss a chance to spend over twenty-four hours of travel—most of them on planes—followed by a week of living in his family's pockets? Of dealing with his brothers. Trying not to feel guilty because he rarely came home, and when he did, couldn't wait to be gone again.

Gladly.

"It wouldn't be the first wedding I've missed," he admitted, dumping the mashed grapes onto the ground and wiping the refractometer on the bottom of his shirt before putting it back into his equipment bag. "I was in France when my eldest brother got hitched. Couldn't make it home in time for the ceremony."

Not that he considered that a great loss. Especially since he and Aidan had a...personality conflict. Matt had a personality while Aidan was a humorless robot. Besides, the marriage hadn't lasted.

Joan crossed her arms. "So if we get a heat wave and the grapes are ready before you're due back..."

"I'll get on the first flight out of the country." He checked his watch. Saw his cushion of two hours before he had to leave for the airport was now down to an hour and a half. And he still had to pack. "Don't worry," he told her as he sat on the ATV and turned the key. "I'll be back before the harvest. You can count on that."

OVER SIXTY HOURS LATER, Matt stood in his brother's cramped kitchen trying to make something edible out of eggs approaching their expiration date and half a loaf of slightly stale, presliced white bread.

He was in hell. Or, as everyone else called it, Jewell, Virginia.

Luckily, it was easy to keep his usual good cheer, thanks to the fact that his time in Jewell would be brief—six days, four hours and fifty-three minutes. Give or take a second or two.

Whistling along with the classic Jackson Browne song playing on the radio, he transferred a soggy slice of bread from the egg and milk mixture in a large bowl to the hot skillet. It sizzled in the greased pan, the scent of cinnamon mingling with that of melted butter. He added a second slice to the pan and took a drink of coffee as a movement to his right caught his attention.

Sporting a seriously bad case of bedhead and wearing a pair of flannel pants with characters from *Family Guy* on them, Brady stood in the open doorway separating the kitchen from the hall.

Matt saluted his brother with his coffee cup. "Morning, Sparky. Nice pj's."

"I'm going to kill you," Brady said in a sleep-roughened voice. His scowl shifted into a thoughtful frown as he sniffed the air. "I'm going to kill you," he repeated, "right after I've had some coffee."

"Can't wait."

Eloquent as usual, Brady grunted and headed toward the coffeemaker, his limp less pronounced than it'd been two months ago when Matt had been home for Christmas.

He flipped the French toast with a fork. "You have any syrup? I didn't see any in the fridge." When he didn't get an answer, he turned to find Brady staring into his coffee cup, his eyes glazed. "If I'm not mistaken— and let's face it, I'm never mistaken—that's the look of a man who recently got lucky. And based on the monkey sounds coming from your room when I got here, I'd say it happened…oh…about twenty minutes ago."

Brady pulled out a chair and sat at the table. "What's the rule about my sex life?"

"It's boring and pathetic?"

"It's not up for discussion."

"Who's discussing it? I was making a simple observation. It's not like I need a play-by-play of whatever it was J.C. did that put that sappy grin on your face."

Brady gave one of his patented *I was a Marine and yes, I will rip your head off and shove that fork down your throat if you say another word* looks.

"Fine." Matt glanced down the hallway to Brady's closed bedroom door. "Uh…you were with J.C., weren't you?" Hey, it was a good question considering that at one time, Brady had been engaged to J.C.'s older sister, Liz.

Brady pinched the bridge of his nose. "Why are you here?"

"Aidan left a message on my cell phone yesterday about a top secret Sheppard brother meeting at eight."

"That's thirty minutes from now. And you're never on time anyway. Especially in the morning."

Matt transferred the cooked French toast to a paper

plate and added more to the pan. "It's ten at night in South Australia."

"You're not in Australia."

No shit. In Australia—and everywhere outside of Jewell—he was a highly respected, highly sought-after vintner.

Here he was the family black sheep.

His fingers tightened around the fork. Too bad his old man hadn't lived long enough to see his youngest son amount to something despite his predictions. Matt forced his fingers to relax. Good thing he'd long ago stopped caring what his family thought of him.

"I'm not in Australia," he said, "but my body thinks I am. And since I was up, I figured I might as well come on over. Once I realized you were otherwise occupied, I decided to make myself at home."

Brady stood and held his hand out. "Give it to me." Matt handed him the plate but his brother shook his head. "No. Give me the spare key."

The spare key their mother kept at her house in case she needed to get into the cottage that sat on the Sheppards' property. The cottage Brady currently occupied.

"You're moving out after the wedding," Matt noted, tossing the plate onto the table. "What's the problem?"

"You let yourself into my house when I was still in bed," Brady said as if Matt was a few grapes shy of a cluster. "You're in my kitchen, blaring music—"

"Only so I couldn't hear all that moaning and groaning coming from your bedroom."

"—making breakfast—"

"For which you should be grateful, seeing as how I made plenty for all of us. That includes J.C."

"Where is it?" Brady asked, his tone low and dangerous.

Matt grinned and patted the front pocket of his jeans. "Right where it's going to stay."

Turning, he flipped the bread. A vise closed around his neck, choking off his amusement. No, not a vise, he realized as Brady yanked him away from the stove, but his brother's forearm. Before Matt could escape, Brady pivoted, clasping his hands together to tighten the headlock.

"The key. Now."

Matt pulled on his brother's arm but it didn't budge. "You want it?" he asked, unable to hide the challenge—or the glee—in his voice. "Go ahead and get it."

Brady squeezed, cutting off the last of Matt's words along with his breath. "I get the key," he said, dragging Matt toward the table, "and you get to walk upright once again. And save what's left of your dignity for getting your ass kicked by a guy with a bum knee."

"Ass kicked?" Matt muttered, doing his damnedest to shake his brother's hold. "I'm taking it easy so I don't hurt you."

"You keep telling yourself that." Then, in a move reminiscent of when they were kids, Brady gave him a quick, rough noogie.

Bum knee or not, the bastard was going down.

Matt grabbed Brady's hip with his right hand while shifting his body to the left. Pushing him off balance, he reached underneath Brady's left leg—conscious of the fact it was his bad leg—and lifted it off the ground.

Brady's arm constricted, cutting into Matt's windpipe. "If I'm going to hit the floor," he warned, "I'm taking you with me."

"Is something burning?"

They froze. J. C. Montgomery padded into the kitchen wearing a pair of pink sweatpants and a long-sleeved brown top stretched to its limit over her pregnant stomach. She wrinkled her nose at what Matt now recognized as the scent of burned French toast, her big brown eyes widening.

"Sorry," Brady said, hopping to maintain his balance. "Did we wake you?"

"That's all right," she said absently, tilting her head to the side to study them. "I hate to ask a stupid question but…is this one of those male bonding things? Because if you two pull out the bongo drums and start chanting, I'll get my phone so I can record it. I'm sure it'll be a huge hit on YouTube."

"We're not bonding," Matt said. "We're fighting. I was just about to drop your fiancé on his head."

"Oh. Well, that makes perfect sense. But since the wedding's in five days, I'd really prefer if he didn't suffer any head injuries. At least until after the ceremony. Besides," she added, "the physical therapist swore Brady will be able to dance with me at our wedding. As long as he doesn't do anything to strain his knee."

She stared at the knee in question—the one in Matt's hands.

Sighing, he let go of his brother. "Killjoy."

"That's me," she said. "A giant fun-suck. How about we arrange a wrestling match for the reception? Maybe one of those cage matches? That is, if I can find a company that rents..." She frowned. "Brady. The fight's over. You can let go of Matt." When he hesitated, she raised her eyebrows. "Now."

He mumbled under his breath, something about dead bolts, alarm systems and idiot brothers, before the pressure around Matt's neck eased.

Slipping out of Brady's hold, Matt smiled at J.C. then took the few steps necessary to cross to her. He gripped her arms. "Good morning, gorgeous."

Then he gave her a smacking kiss on the cheek.

As he eased back, Brady growled. It made Matt want to kiss J.C. again.

"Uh...good morning to you, too." She peeked around his shoulder at Brady. "You never told me your family was so...affectionate in the morning."

"He just did that to piss me off," Brady said.

"Not true," Matt claimed. "Though that's a nice side benefit. But the truth is," he continued, lowering his voice and leaning closer to J.C., "I'm weak. I have a hard time resisting a beautiful woman."

She blushed and attempted to smooth her wildly curling mane of dark hair. Damn, but she was a sweetheart.

Brady had somehow hit the jackpot. That is, if you considered being tied to one woman for the rest of your life winning big.

Brady cleared his throat. "If you're done flirting with my fiancée, you might want to check your breakfast. It's on fire."

With a wink at J.C., Matt went back to the stove. There weren't any flames, just a lot of thick smoke. Matt flipped the burner to low while Brady opened the small window over the sink.

After he dumped the burned food into the garbage can, Matt unwound several paper towels from the roll, balled them up and wiped out the pan before setting it back on the burner. "How about some French toast?" he asked J.C., adding fresh butter to the pan.

She looked up from pouring herself a large glass of orange juice. "You don't have to cook for me. I can fix some—"

"It's the least I can do."

"He's got that right," Brady muttered.

"Well," J.C. said as she picked the fork Matt had dropped earlier off the floor, "if you really don't mind…"

"Honey, I never mind cooking breakfast for a woman."

She smiled. "In that case, I'd love some."

In less than ten minutes, Matt made what he considered enough French toast to feed a family of five. Or at least two grown men and one pregnant lady. By the time the food was ready, Brady had donned a shirt and he and J.C. had paper plates, forks, an unopened container of syrup and a stick of butter still in its wrapper on the table.

They'd started eating when Aidan came into the kitchen, his blond hair neatly trimmed, his dark slacks crisply pleated. "Morning," he said to the room at large as he went to the coffeepot and poured himself a cup. He took a sip, his eyes on Matt. "I didn't think you'd bother showing up until at least eight-thirty."

Giving himself time to hide a quick burst of irritation, Matt swallowed the food in his mouth. Just like their father, Aidan always thought the worst of him. "Hey, you know I'm happy to obey your orders."

"Why, what time is it?" J.C. asked, sounding panicked. Before any of them could reply, she grabbed Matt's hand and twisted it so she could read his watch. "Crap. I'm late." Leaping to her feet, she drained her juice glass. "I'm supposed to meet Mrs. Wertz in ten minutes for my last dress fitting."

"Don't you have the day off?" Brady asked.

"Yes, but she doesn't, and I asked her to squeeze me in before she goes to work. Thanks for breakfast," she called before rushing out of the room. A moment later, the front door banged shut.

Matt scratched his cheek. "Does she realize it's barely thirty degrees out and she's not wearing any shoes or a coat?"

Brady held his forefinger up. Five seconds later, the front door opened and J.C. sped past them. When she came back through a minute later, her sweatpants were tucked into a pair of boots and she was zipping up a bulky, shapeless coat, her purse hanging off her elbow.

And once again, the door slammed shut.

"One thing's for sure," Matt said as he snagged the last piece of French toast. "Your life isn't going to be boring."

Aidan sat in the seat J.C. had vacated. "Since we're all here, let's get right to it."

Matt snorted as he doused his toast with syrup. Right. Wouldn't want to waste time with small talk even if he hadn't spoken to either of his brothers for over two months. His mother being the only family he'd seen since he'd been back this time. "If this is about Brady's stag party," he said, "I've already hired the strippers."

"We want to talk to you about the Diamond Dust," Aidan said, sliding the remnants of J.C.'s breakfast aside before setting his cup down. He wrapped his hands around the mug. "We want you with us."

"I'm right here, aren't I?"

"We want you working with us at the winery. We want you to be our partner."

Matt stilled, his fork halfway to his mouth. His throat constricted. Partners? With his brothers? "Why would I want to do that?"

"Told you," Brady said, leaning back in his chair, his hands linked on his stomach.

Aidan kept his hooded eyes on Matt. "Why wouldn't you?"

He slowly lowered his fork back to his plate. "I already have a career."

A damned good one, too, not that his brothers ever bothered to mention it. His reputation as a winemaker and consultant was growing and, after he led Queen's Valley to success, so would the number of wineries who wanted to hire him. He'd have his pick of jobs all over the world. And his brothers thought he'd give that up to stay in tiny Jewell to take over his father's business?

"Instead of making wine for other people," Aidan said, "you'd be making it for your own company. Your own label. And you'd have a chance to put down roots."

Put down roots? The back of his neck broke out in a cold sweat. "Thanks but when I do decide to settle in one place—" if he ever decided to settle in one place "—I'd rather it be Italy or France or Napa Valley."

"Dad's dream was to pass the Diamond Dust down to his sons," Aidan said quietly. "All three of us."

Matt tipped his chair back until it balanced on two legs. His father had hated when he did that. "Dad's gone. And like you said, that was his dream. Not mine. And as far as I can remember, it wasn't either one of your dreams, either."

"Things change."

True. But Matt hadn't changed. He'd never wanted to be stuck in Jewell working at the Diamond Dust. Working for his overly critical, rigid father. And while Tom Sheppard might be gone, the worst parts of his personality lived on in his eldest son. The tight leash his dad had tried to keep him on when he was growing up had almost choked Matt to death. He wasn't about to put on another one.

"Sorry," he said as he stood, "but I'm not interested."

"Tell him," Brady murmured to Aidan.

His scalp tingled. His pulse pounded in his ears. "Tell me what?"

Jaw tight, Aidan slowly got to his feet. "You have to partner with us—move back to Jewell and help run the winery. If you don't, Mom's going to sell the Diamond Dust to someone else."

CHAPTER TWO

IT WAS A JOKE. SOME SORT of elaborate prank. It had to be.

Matt hunched his shoulders against the cold morning breeze and closed the front door of his mom's house. The Diamond Dust meant too much to his mother for her to just toss it aside like it was an old sweater that didn't fit her anymore.

Besides, he'd been home almost two days and she hadn't once mentioned anything about selling the winery to him.

How could she not have told him before?

Shoving his hands into his jacket pockets, he headed down the winding road hoping to catch her on the way back from her daily walk—and to give himself time to work off some of his building irritation. He didn't want to face her until he'd gotten this surge of unreasonable panic under control.

He passed between a large block of Cabernet Franc vines and some Nortons—plants he and Brady had helped their father put in over fifteen years ago. The sun rose above the hills to his right, splashing light on the bare trees, illuminating the frost on the ground. Ten minutes later, his nose freezing, his ears stinging with

cold, he reached the farmhouse which had been exten-
sively renovated to house the Diamond Dust's gift shop
and tasting room. Just beyond it was the actual winery,
a building designed to match the weathered exterior of
the farmhouse but with a large cellar for making and
storing the wine.

Frowning, he stared across the empty parking lot then
narrowed his eyes as he studied the rows of vines in the
number ten block. Or was it number eleven? Either way,
they hadn't even been pruned yet, which was a mistake
since it was the middle of February. And they really
should install a drip irrigation…

He ground his back teeth together. Whoa. Back up
there, hotshot. None of that was his concern. And by
God, he was going to keep it that way.

A dog barked. Matt glanced over to see Aidan's Irish
setter, Lily, keeping pace beside his mother as they came
around the bend.

"Have you lost your mind?" he asked.

"What was that?" Not slowing, she reached under
the wide, white headband covering her short cap of hair
and pulled a set of headphones away from her ears. He
noticed the small MP3 player hooked to her pocket.
Good to see she was using the birthday gift he'd given
her.

"I asked if you'd lost your mind."

The sun picked out the gray strands in her dark blond
hair as her arms pumped furiously at her sides, the shiny,
dark blue material of her windbreaker swishing softly.
"If I had, would I even be aware of it?"

He took hold of her elbow, forcing her to stop. "Did you threaten to sell the Diamond Dust to a third party if Aidan, Brady and I don't agree to take over?"

He held his breath while she squinted up at him from behind her glasses, the lines around her eyes prominent. "I wouldn't call it a threat."

He dropped her arm, his stomach sinking. "What would you call it?"

"An opportunity."

"What the hell is that supposed to mean?"

"Do not raise your voice to me, Matthew," she said in an all-too-familiar tone. "If you can't discuss this in a calm, reasonable manner, then there's nothing more to say."

"You're trying to ruin my life and you want me to be reasonable?"

"For your information," she said so coldly it made the morning temperatures feel practically balmy, "this is not some evil plot geared toward the destruction of your happiness."

Sure seemed that way to him.

"Wait a minute," he said, starting to pace, "was this Al's idea?" Retired Senator Al Wallace, his mother's fiancé, seemed like a nice enough guy, but Matt had only met him a few times. Somehow he couldn't fathom his mother coming up with this idea on her own.

"Of course not. Al only wants me to be happy." She exhaled heavily, her breath forming a soft cloud. "I've just realized it's…it's time for me to step back from the Diamond Dust."

"So step back," he said, wincing at how desperate he sounded. "You want to retire? Fine. Go on and move to D.C. after you get married. Aidan and Brady can keep the winery running."

"They could," she agreed. "But, Matt, I'm not going to be around forever—"

"Oh, for God's sake," he muttered.

"—and I want to make sure the winery is in good hands. Aidan and Brady need a quality vintner's expertise if they want to do more than simply keep the winery afloat. I see no reason to drag this out. Especially when I have interest from a prospective buyer."

He stopped and gaped at her. "What?"

"An old friend of Al's contacted me last week. He asked if I was considering retiring since Al and I were engaged. Seems he, along with his daughter and son-in-law, are interested in purchasing an established winery and he thinks the Diamond Dust would be a good fit for them." She sent him a pitying glance. "Didn't your brothers explain all of this?"

"Guess they left a few details out."

Like the most important fact of all. Instead, Brady had, according to his usual M.O., remained silent while Aidan had gone on about their responsibility to their heritage and their father's memory. Neither one had mentioned there was a real live buyer interested in the winery.

Matt shoved his numb fingers into his pockets. "Being interested isn't the same as having an offer on the table."

She gave him her, *do you really think I'm an idiot?* look, the one she'd used when he'd been fifteen and had tried to sneak out of the house with two bottles of wine tucked inside his jacket.

"He's already made a substantial initial offer on the business."

"How substantial?" he asked, not sure he wanted to hear the answer.

She tipped her head to the side. "Fourteen point five."

His mouth fell open. He shut it. Opened it again "As in…million?" She nodded. "Just for the winery?" He'd known the Diamond Dust was profitable but he'd never have guessed it did that well.

"For the business, the property and buildings."

His head snapped back as if she'd slapped him. "Buildings? You'd sell the plantation? Our house?"

For a moment he thought she'd deny it but then her lips thinned. "I could hardly sell one without the other. The Diamond Dust is the plantation and vice versa."

His stomach turned. No wonder the offer was huge. The Diamond Dust was over three hundred acres of rolling hills and dense woods set just on the outskirts of Jewell. Sixty of those three hundred acres were planted vineyards. Add those in with the five buildings on the property and you had some seriously prime real estate.

And his mother didn't just plan to unload the business she'd spent most of her life building, she also wanted to sell the land that had been in the Sheppard family for over one hundred and fifty years. Un-freaking-believable.

"Who has that kind of money, especially in this real estate market?" he asked. "Wait, it's not Donald Trump, is it?"

"Of course not," she said, as if he was the one who'd lost his mind instead of her. "It's Lester Caldwell."

With a short bark of laughter, Matt tipped his head back. Lester Caldwell. Make that Lt. Governor Lester Caldwell, the son of a prominent Virginia family and a successful businessman in his own right. A man who was well connected and had more money than he could ever spend in three lifetimes. Who had a reputation for getting what he wanted. And if he wanted the Diamond Dust, Matt didn't doubt he'd even blink at spending twice what the winery was worth.

Damn politicians.

"If this is about money, I can help you out." He did a quick mental review of his bank accounts. "Give me a few days, a week at the most, to get some funds moved around and I'll cut you a check."

She squeezed his hand. "That's generous, honey, but it's not about the money."

He stepped back. "No," he said, unable to keep the resentment out of his voice. "It's about Dad. You're doing this for him. To fulfill his dream of having all his sons work here."

They stared at each other. Lily barked, either at the tension surrounding them or at the squirrel scurrying up a tree.

"Yes. I'm doing this for him." This time when she spoke, there was no hesitation, no doubt in her voice. "His only dream was to someday see his sons—all three sons—run the winery. When Aidan chose law school and Brady enlisted and you...left...he gave up that dream. And then he got sick...." She shook her head. Sighed. "I know this is hard for you to understand, but I'm only doing what I think is best. For everyone involved, especially you and your brothers."

He fisted his hands. "Don't drag me into this. They want the winery. I don't."

"Sometimes a parent has to make difficult decisions. Decisions that her children may not understand, even though they're in their best interest."

Bitterness filled him. Forcing him into doing something he never wanted any part of was in *her* best interest. Aidan and Brady were already on board, doing exactly what Tom Sheppard had always hoped—living in Jewell. Devoting their lives to the Diamond Dust.

Aidan had taken over the winery when their father got sick. When Tom died, Aidan had quit law school and moved back to Jewell, a choice that guaranteed the end of his own dreams. And his short-lived marriage.

A few months back, Brady had started working at the winery, too. Since he was rarely home, Matt didn't have all the inside info on exactly how that had transpired, but he figured Brady must've been pretty damned desperate to accept a job where Aidan would be his boss.

No wonder their mom had come up with this crazy blackmail scheme. She was already two-thirds of the way to getting exactly what her husband had always wanted. But there was just one loose end.

Him.

"I'm not doing it," he said, his voice harsh, his jaw tight. "I have a three-year contract with Queen's Valley. I made a commitment to them. I can't just break it."

She clasped her hands together in front of her. "I realize that each of you may have to give something up in order to take over the Diamond Dust, and I'm sorry for that. I truly am. But there would never be a perfect time for this, and with Lester's offer on the table…" She shrugged, as if his career, his reputation and everything he'd worked for since leaving Jewell ten years ago meant less than nothing. "I can't afford to wait."

"You're bluffing," he said softly, watching her reaction carefully. Her expression didn't change. "There's no way you'd ever sell the winery—not to mention our home and the Sheppard legacy—to strangers just to force me back to the Diamond Dust."

"I'd think you would have learned one thing by now, Matthew." She drew herself up to her full height—and though he had at least eight inches on her, it still seemed as if she was peering down her nose at him. "I never bluff." She brushed past him only to stop and glance over her shoulder. "I'll expect your answer by 5:00 p.m. Tonight."

"MOMMY, SHE WON'T GIVE my Barbie back!"

Standing on the stoop of the two-story brick home that had been converted into offices for the Diamond

Dust, Connie Henkel winced at her younger daughter's whining. Honestly, it was enough to make a person's ears bleed.

She glanced around to make sure no one else had suffered permanent hearing damage. Thankfully, they were alone. No cars were parked in front of the office building or the Sheppards' large, plantation-style home, which sat just over a hundred yards away. The surrounding blocks of vineyard were set against a backdrop of rolling hills, bare except for clusters of dull green pine trees.

Her vines weren't green. Dormant, conserving energy throughout the cold winter months, they were brown and straggly, their crooked, frost-covered, entwined limbs reaching for the sun. Soon they would come back to life. It was up to her and her workers to make sure they thrived.

And she was damn good at her job.

Shifting the folder she held to her other hand, she turned the doorknob, frowning to find it locked. That was weird. Brady usually beat her to work. And more importantly, started the coffee. And if ever there was a morning when she could use the extra kick of caffeine, today was it. After unlocking the door, she stood aside to let her two daughters into the small entryway. Neither one of them moved.

Abby, the brim of her lavender fleece hat pulled down to her eyebrows, stomped her foot. "Mommy!"

Right. Barbie doll kidnapping. Major crisis. Intervention needed from Supermom.

She was on it.

"Payton, give your sister her doll," Connie said. See? She really was Supermom. How else could she have spoken with such restraint, such remarkable calm, if not for her super powers? After all, a mere mortal would've lost her patience by now, considering this was the fifth argument between her two daughters this morning. And it wasn't even 9:00 a.m.

God help her. She didn't think she'd make it to ten o'clock without yanking her own hair out.

Eight-year-old Payton swept past her with all the dignity of a four-foot-tall queen, the doll clutched in her gloved hand. "But I still have five minutes left. I let her listen to my iPod for fifteen minutes. So that's how long I get her Barbie."

"But I want her back now," Abby wailed, her gray eyes filling with tears.

"Yeah?" Connie asked. "Well, I want you to come inside so I can close the door."

"But, Mom—"

"Now."

Funny. As soon as she'd become a mother, she'd been able to inject a wealth of meaning into one tiny word. Abby, being no dummy, heard the implied threat of loss of privileges if she didn't obey and scurried inside.

Connie shut the door then crouched so she was eye to eye with her unhappy daughter. "Sorry, kid, but a deal's a deal. You'll get Barbie back in a few minutes. Until then, you're just going to have to be patient."

Abby's face scrunched up as if this development

was a fate worse than the Disney Channel being removed from their cable company's lineup. Her head hanging, her toy-filled backpack dragging on the floor, she trudged down the dark hall toward Connie's office. Payton, smug in her victory, swung poor Barbie by her hair as she followed.

Connie hung her heavy work coat on the antique rack in the corner. Tucking the folder under her arm, she passed Brady's empty office and a small half bath, then entered the narrow kitchen and got a Diet Coke out of the refrigerator.

The building was over a hundred years old with dark, ornate woodwork, wide-planked floors and high ceilings. While the first floor was converted into office space, the second had been kept as bedrooms for seasonal workers who needed a place to stay. Since the winery was nearing the end of its off-season, the bedrooms were currently empty, but within a matter of weeks she planned on hiring at least half a dozen workers to help plant new vines.

Popping the tab on the can, she took a drink as she made her way to her office at the back of the building. No sooner did she step into the room than Abby flounced onto the brick-red sofa, her long, dark brown ponytail swinging with the momentum. She sent Connie a defiant look and stuck her thumb in her mouth.

Connie shut her eyes. That was it. Her next husband was going to be an orthodontist. It was the only way she'd ever be able to pay to have Abby's bite corrected.

Too bad the only orthodontist in town was sixty years old. And a woman.

Taking another sip of her soda so she wouldn't snap at her daughter about her thumb-sucking, she set the folder on the glossy surface of her maple desk and sat back in her leather, ergonomic chair. Diane Sheppard had decorated Connie's office. The cream-colored beadboard below chocolate walls, hardwood floor and built-in bookcases gave the room warmth and charm.

"I'm bored," Payton grumbled.

"The two most dreaded words on the planet," Connie murmured as she turned on her laptop. "How will you ever survive?"

Payton tossed the doll over to her sister, who clutched it to her chest as if Barbie had just returned from war. "Mom, I'm serious."

"Payton," Connie said, mimicking her daughter's exasperated tone, "so am I. Read your book."

"I don't feel like reading," she said, glancing derisively at the copy of *The Lightning Thief* next to her.

"Then maybe you should've brought something else to keep you occupied."

"If we could've brought the dollhouse, I wouldn't be bored," she muttered.

Right. Lug the three-foot-tall, sixteen-room monstrosity—complete with furnishings—across town? "Yeah, well, that didn't happen, did it?"

"Daddy would've let me."

At her daughter's challenging tone, Connie jabbed the delete key, ridding herself of an email touting the secret to getting a larger penis. "I'm sure he would have. But he's not here. I am."

Paul, her ex-husband, felt so guilty about not being able to see the girls as often as he'd like that he and his too-good-to-be-true second wife, Sarah, let them do whatever they wanted, whenever they wanted. Every time Payton and Abby came back from their once-a-month weekend visits with their father, it took Connie almost a week to deprogram them from acting like mini prima donnas.

The front door opened and shut. "Hello?" a familiar voice called. "Anyone here?"

"In my office," Connie said, sliding the folder she'd set on her desk into the top drawer. Yeah, it was stupid to feel nervous or, worse, embarrassed by the information she'd put together, but she felt both just the same.

"I thought I saw your car pull in," Diane Sheppard said from the doorway, her chin-length hair windblown and her cheeks pink from the walk across the yard. "What's this? No school today?"

Abby scrambled off the couch and wrapped her arm around Diane's leg. "Nuh-uh. It's President's Day."

"And you get the day off?" Diane asked, as if President's Day was some new and exciting development. "Since it honors two very important men, we should celebrate it, don't you think?"

"Like a party?" Payton asked.

"Exactly like a party. Why don't we go over to the house and make plans over some hot cocoa?" Keeping a hand on each of the girls' shoulders, she smiled at

Connie. "You don't mind if I steal them for a little bit, do you?"

Mind? She had to stop herself from begging Diane to do just that. She had pruning to start, a job that could take her small crew of three anywhere from a few weeks to an entire month. Plus, she had to go over the results of the soil sample she'd sent out last week for the new block of land she wanted to plant this spring.

Abby clapped her hands. "Can we, Mommy?"

"Please?" Payton added, pushing her glasses back with one finger.

"You two have been at each other's throats all morning," Connie was forced to point out. After all, the girls weren't Diane's responsibility. No matter how much work Connie had to do. "I couldn't, in good conscience, subject Diane to your whining and fighting."

"We won't fight," Payton said, and then she pulled Abby into a hug.

Abby nodded vigorously, her head bumping Payton's chin. "See? We're best friends again."

"It's a President's Day miracle," Connie murmured.

"I raised three boys," Diane said. "I think I can handle a little bit of whining and fighting. Besides, if we're going to throw an impromptu party, I'll need their help."

"You need help planning a party like the Pope needs help praying." Connie crossed her arms and realized her burgundy scarf was still wrapped around her neck. Unwinding it, she narrowed her eyes at her boss. "You know, it is possible for the girls to keep themselves occupied while I'm here. You don't have to entertain them every time I bring them with me to work."

"I realize that," Diane said with a wave of her fingers, as if she didn't find some excuse to take the girls off Connie's hands whenever she could.

The sunlight filtering through the picture window caught on Diane's new engagement ring, making the large, square-cut diamond sparkle. Even though she wore the ring of another man, a man she planned to marry in a few short months, Diane hadn't removed the wedding band and engagement ring from her first husband. She'd just shifted them to her right hand.

Connie rubbed the pad of her thumb against the base of her ring finger. She hadn't felt anything when she'd taken her wedding ring off four years ago. Well, except relief. She'd wanted to feel more. Sadness. Loss. Anger. Even a sense of failure would've sufficed. Instead, she'd remained numb.

Maybe she really was as cold and unfeeling as Paul had accused her of being.

"Please, Mommy," Payton repeated. "We'll be really good."

"And we'll help Diane a whole lot," Abby piped in.

"Okay, okay. Stop with the begging already. You can go. Stay as long as Diane wants you, but you—" she pointed at Diane "—need to promise me you'll send them right back here if they misbehave."

Diane adjusted the barrette in Payton's wavy, light brown hair. "Of course."

Connie rolled her eyes. The only way her kids would

be sent back was if they set the kitchen on fire. And even that wasn't a guarantee.

"Come on, girls." Diane zipped up Abby's coat even though she was more than capable of doing it on her own. "We have lots of work if we're having a party today."

When they were gone, Connie swiveled in her chair to watch them through the window as they crossed the brown grass toward the house. Abby held Diane's hand while Payton skipped ahead. Aidan's Irish setter, Lily, bounded out of the woods, joining the group.

It was a picture-perfect scene, one straight out of a hokey holiday commercial. Like they were all one big happy family.

Which they were. Sort of. They belonged here, she and her girls. And there was one way to make it permanent.

Her stomach rolling, she tugged open the top drawer and pulled out the folder with the plan she'd outlined showing Aidan why they should partner up and take over the Diamond Dust.

It was a crazy idea but one she hadn't been able to shake since Christmas Eve when Diane got engaged and mentioned that she wanted to retire in the near future. And when that happened, who better to take over than Connie and Aidan? They were the ones who'd been with the winery ever since Tom got sick. Who loved it as much as he had.

Nerves and excitement dancing in her stomach, Connie pulled her cell phone from her pocket and dialed Aidan's number before she changed her mind.

When he picked up after two rings, she cleared her throat. "Hey, it's me," she said. "Do you have any free time this morning? I need to talk to you about something important."

CHAPTER THREE

STILL FUMING OVER HIS conversation with his mother, Matt walked into Aidan's office only to skid to a stop as if he was a dog and had reached the end of his leash. "What is this, the Tom Sheppard shrine?"

Sitting behind their father's enormous desk, Aidan didn't even look up. "I'm working."

Matt shook his head as he slowly took in the large room. A room he'd managed to avoid since his father's death.

But why did it look exactly as it had when Tom was still alive? Same dark colors, oppressive furniture and—he narrowed his eyes—was that...yeah...same ugly bronze frog on the bottom shelf of the built-in bookcase.

"I hate this room," he muttered.

"How can you hate a room?" Aidan asked as he continued to work on a financial report or inventory sheet or some such mind-numbingly boring item.

"If I ever end up behind that desk, do me a favor and just shoot me."

He did hate this room. Not just the decorating, although if he ever got stuck playing desk jockey, he wanted a space that was all his. Not someone else's leftovers. No, what he really hated about his father's office was that stepping into the room was like stepping back in time. He couldn't count the number of times his father had called him in here only to rip him up one side and down the other. Hell, he'd spent most of his teenage years slouched in the leather chair across from the desk, forced to listen to his old man lecture about responsibility, making good choices and the importance of doing his best no matter what the situation.

All important lessons, Matt acknowledged grudgingly. And ones he deserved to hear, just as he probably deserved most of the punishments his father had doled out in response to his youngest son's wild ways.

Then again, maybe if Tom hadn't been such a hard-ass, Matt wouldn't have rebelled so much.

Aidan finally set his mechanical pencil down. "Don't tell me, you hate that chair, too." When Matt raised an eyebrow, Aidan continued, "You look like you're ready to rip it apart with your teeth."

That was why he'd avoided this room ever since his dad died. It was too full of memories. And memories only caused problems. Better to focus on the present. And the current hell he was living through.

"We need to discuss this…situation we're in," Matt said, keeping his tone neutral.

"I take it you're referring to our conversation earlier, the one that caused you to take off like the devil himself was riding your ass."

He'd rather deal with the devil. Old Satan had nothing on Aidan Sheppard. "I needed some fresh air. Time to clear my head. I went back to the cottage but you'd already left."

Aidan leaned back in his chair. "Once again, I'm working. Some of us can't get by logging in twenty hours a week then heading off to climb some mountain or jump off a cliff."

He wished his brother would jump off a cliff. Preferably without a bungee cord. So what if he took time off now and again? Life was an adventure. One he planned on getting the most out of.

Matt shoved his hands into his pockets and walked to the window to stare out over the backyard. But that didn't mean he didn't take his jobs seriously. His family had no idea what his life was really like. Up at 4:00 a.m., logging up to eighty hours a week in order to help the wineries who hired him produce the best wines possible.

"I realize your time is valuable—more so than that of us mere working stiffs," Matt said, "but I'd think you could spare a few minutes to discuss the future of the Diamond Dust." He faced his brother, leaning back against the wall. "What's Mom trying to prove?"

"You'd have to ask her."

"I did. She admitted she's doing this for Dad. I bet he put some stipulation in his will so this would happen." Matt wouldn't put it past the old man. Even dead he was trying to run Matt's life.

"He didn't."

"How do you know?"

"Because I, unlike you or Brady, was actually there

for the reading of Dad's will," Aidan said. "Trust me, this is all Mom's idea."

Matt fisted his hands. The betrayal was like a punch to the chest. Why would she do this to him? They'd always been close. She'd been the one person he could count on to see the real him. She'd known, better than anyone, how badly he'd wanted to escape Jewell. How he'd wanted nothing more than to go out and make something of himself. Something important.

He crossed to the leather sofa against the opposite wall. Guess her reasons didn't really matter. Not when all he could do now was deal with this situation.

"So what's it going to be?" Aidan asked.

Matt lay down, propping his feet on the armrest. "I need time to think it through."

"We don't have time. Mom wants our decision today."

"Yeah, she told me. Eight hours to decide my entire future? How generous."

"Suck it up. Some of us only got five minutes."

True. Aidan had to drop out of law school and move back to Jewell to take over the Diamond Dust when their father passed away. And Brady's plans had been altered when he'd lost his fiancée to some other guy and his career to an injury sustained in Afghanistan. Both Aidan's and Brady's futures had taken turns neither had expected, but that didn't make the possible annihilation of his own plans any easier to swallow. Especially since they both seemed to be doing fine now.

"Well, since I do have eight hours, I'm going to take

them. I'll let you know my decision then." Maybe he could talk his mother out of this insane idea before tonight. Or at least get her to agree to let him be a partner in name only. There had to be a way out of this.

His jet lag catching up to him, he linked his fingers behind his head and closed his eyes. It wasn't much time and he had a lot to think about. Damn it, he had plans. Commitments. His reputation as a world-class vintner was growing—the proof was his contract with Queen's Valley.

But as much as he didn't want to be in Jewell, he also didn't want to see his father's business sold to some stranger.

More than that, he didn't want to let his brothers down.

And he'd French-kiss Aidan's dog before he admitted that out loud.

He yawned. His brothers might think he slid by in life, but the truth was, he'd busted his ass building his reputation as a winemaker. He wasn't afraid of hard work, and along the way he'd learned from some of the best experts in the world how to run a winery.

He just didn't want to use that knowledge to run the Diamond Dust.

"I have a proposition for you."

Matt's eyes flew open at the husky feminine voice. Too bad he wasn't the one being propositioned. Which was probably a good thing, he realized, as Connie Henkel walked past him without so much as a glance.

She was long and lean with sharp features, and her

dark hair was cut shorter than his, with messy layers on top and wisps around her ears. She didn't wear jewelry or makeup, and in her usual uniform of faded jeans and a T-shirt, if you didn't take the time to look carefully, she could've passed for a teenage boy.

One side of his mouth kicked up. Luckily, Matt always looked carefully. So he noticed the subtle curve of her hips, the slight rise and fall of her small breasts, the feminine arch of her dark brows.

He noticed, he just didn't linger.

"I'm not sure whether to be flattered," Aidan said, "or terrified."

Connie winced. "First of all…eww. You're like the brother I never had and never particularly wanted. And second of all, if you were that lucky, you wouldn't be terrified. You'd be grateful."

Quietly sitting up, Matt couldn't help but grin. He'd always enjoyed Connie's smart-ass ways. "I'd sure be grateful if it was me." He winked at her. "And believe me, so would you."

Connie didn't move. Her face was white, her mouth open. Hell, she didn't even blink.

It was that blank stare and the fact that he'd known Connie since he was twelve and he'd never seen her stay still for more than a few seconds that had Matt standing and walking toward her. "You okay?" he asked. "You're not having some sort of seizure or anything, are you?"

And just like that, she snapped back to life. Before

he could decipher the play of emotions across her face, she smiled, though it seemed forced.

"Hey. I didn't know you were in town." She stepped forward as if to give him a hug, only to tuck her hands, and the bright purple folder she held, behind her back.

"Got in Saturday night," he said, leaning against Aidan's desk, his hip hitting a pile of papers and causing them to slide. He could've sworn he heard Aidan muttering under his breath. Knowing it would drive his brother crazy, Matt slowly slid his gaze over Connie. "Did you miss me?"

"It was all I could do to get through each day," she said somberly.

Even with the weight of his pending decision on his chest, making it difficult to take a full breath, he couldn't help but enjoy her. "What say we leave Aidan to his paperwork and go catch up over a cup of coffee?"

What better way to pretend his entire future wasn't on the line than with the distraction of a smart, funny, attractive woman?

"You're embarrassing yourself," Aidan said before Connie could respond. "Besides, Connie has something she wants to discuss with me, so why don't—"

"No," she blurted, her cheeks turning pink when he and Aidan stared at her. Taking a step back, she cleared her throat. "I mean…that…that was nothing. The thing I wanted to discuss. It can wait."

"Are you sure?" Aidan asked.

"Believe me, I'm positive. I don't want to interrupt your discussion so I'll just go."

And she turned and walked out.

"How do you do that?" Aidan asked.

Matt watched Connie's backside as she walked away. "Do what?"

"Flirt with my vineyard manager when I know what you really want is to rip someone's head off."

Straightening, he shrugged, making sure the gesture seemed casual despite the tightness in his shoulders. "None of this is Connie's fault," he said, heading back to the sofa. "Why take it out on her?"

Never let them see you sweat.

He lay down again and closed his eyes, shutting out the searching look Aidan was giving him. His brother's unspoken questions. Matt knew what his family thought of him. How they perceived him. To them he was just a charming playboy—albeit one with a small amount of talent. Talent he used when he wasn't busy white-water rafting, mountain climbing or seducing women.

All he did was give them what they wanted to see.

COWARD.

Connie slowly descended the stairs, the folder with her proposal bent in her clenched hand. So she'd chickened out. Who could blame her? She could hardly be expected to pitch a business deal to Aidan while Matt flirted with her.

Not that she took him seriously. He flirted with every female regardless of her looks or age. But him being there had thrown her.

And made her lose her nerve.

Crap.

It was probably for the best. This way she could take a few more days, look over her proposal. Make sure it was as good as it needed to be to convince Aidan to take her on as a partner.

As if tweaking the damn thing for the past eight weeks wasn't enough.

She sighed. Yeah, she really was a coward.

In the foyer, she made a right turn, her steps slowing as the sound of her daughters' laughter reached her.

She inhaled for the count of five then exhaled heavily before stepping into the kitchen. "Something smells good," she said, forcing a smile.

"We're making cinnamon rolls," Abby said, not looking up from the dough Diane was helping her roll out.

"And look, Mommy." Payton held up a metal bowl filled with what appeared to be brown sugar. "I made the filling all by myself. And I get to sprinkle it over the dough, too."

Abby straightened. "I get to pour the melted butter over it, don't I, Diane?"

Diane straightened and used a towel to wipe flour from Abby's cheek. "You certainly do."

Payton jumped off the stool and raced over to the refrigerator. "And did you see? Diane put our thank-you cards on the fridge."

There, in the middle of the shiny stainless steel, held on by round magnets, were the handmade cards Payton and Abby had made to thank her for the Christmas gifts she'd given them.

"I put them there because all works of art should be displayed," Diane said, stretching the dough by hand into a large rectangle.

Connie got a heavy red mug from the cupboard next to the refrigerator and filled it with coffee. She leaned back against the counter and watched Diane instruct Payton on how to sprinkle the brown sugar mixture over the dough.

"Is everything all right?" Diane asked her. "Is it your mom?"

Connie shook her head. "Everything's fine. Mom's fine. I spoke with her earlier and she sounded good."

Diane patted her cheek. "I'm glad to hear it. But you know if you ever need me for anything, to take her to a doctor's appointment or to watch the girls for you, you just let me know."

"I will. Thanks." A lump formed in Connie's throat. She took a swallow of too-hot coffee to wash it away. "I just came from Aidan's office and saw Matt there."

"You make it sound like you just ran into the Loch Ness monster."

"Well, it was a…rare sighting." She frowned. "Come to think of it, I can't remember seeing Matt up there since Tom died."

"All my boys dealt with their father's death in their own way," she said, her voice taking on that note of grief, of longing it always did when she spoke of her deceased husband. "Aidan couldn't bear to change anything in that office to keep the memories alive, while

Matt avoided both the room and the feelings those memories evoked."

"And Brady?"

"Brady went off to war, away from us all." She crossed over to the stove and unwrapped a stick of butter before putting it in a small saucepan. "Who's to say any of them were wrong?"

Well, Connie could say. After all, Brady and Matt had left Aidan and Diane when they needed them most. But, she thought with no little amount of pride, she'd been there. For them and for the Diamond Dust.

Finishing her coffee, she rinsed the cup in the sink. "I'd better get back to work."

"Why don't I bring the girls over to you after lunch?" Diane asked.

"That's fine. I'll be out in Pinot Noir block if you need me. You two behave," she told her daughters.

"We will," Abby assured her. "Bye, Mommy."

Connie went out the back door. There was no way she was going to take the chance of running into Aidan or Matt again. It wasn't until she was safely back in her office with the door shut that she realized she was still carrying the folder with her proposal.

She laid it on her neat desk. God, it was almost laughable. She'd spent half her life wanting nothing more than to be a part of the Diamond Dust, to be a member of the Sheppard family, and she was too scared to go for it.

For sixteen years she'd worked hard to prove her loyalty to both the family and the winery. To prove her worth. When Tom lost his battle with pancreatic cancer, she was the one who'd helped Aidan make the transition to winery president. Matt and Brady had both been long gone, but she'd stuck. And she'd busted her ass to keep the Diamond Dust going.

Connie snorted. Who knew? Maybe her mother had been right all this time. Maybe she really did need to stop wishing for things that weren't going to happen. That weren't meant to be.

She sat down, and after a moment, put the folder back in the bottom drawer.

"CAN'T YOU DO SOMETHING that will guarantee he'll agree?" Diane asked Aidan later that day as they waited for Brady and Matt in her large kitchen.

"No problem." Aidan sat at the table, tipped his head side to side in an effort to ease the tension tightening his muscles. "If Matt shows up, I'll put him in a choke hold so you can point a gun to his head."

Diane's mouth flattened into a disapproving line. "I'm being serious, Aidan."

He drummed his fingers where a shaft of sunlight hit the table through sliding glass doors that led to a bricked veranda. "We both know Matt will draw this out for as long as possible. You didn't really think he'd go along with this idea willingly, did you? Or make it easy on any of us?"

"A mother can hope," she murmured, wiping non-existent crumbs from the granite kitchen counter with a dishcloth. She scrubbed at a spot by the stove. "Is it so wrong for me to want my sons, all three of my sons, working together?"

And that question was as loaded as the hypothetical gun Aidan had just mentioned. "What if one of those sons doesn't want to be a part of the Diamond Dust?"

"Matt wants to be a part of it." Crossing to the opposite wall, she wiped fingerprints from one of the double, stainless steel ovens. "He just doesn't realize it yet. Just as Brady didn't realize it until you convinced him."

Convinced? Aidan rose and walked over to the fridge. Lily, who'd been napping in front of the large stone fireplace in the connecting family room, padded over to him, her nails clicking on the tile floor. He hadn't convinced his brother to do anything, he thought as he got a can of soda. Nothing short of dynamite could move Brady once he'd set his mind to stay still. A trait all the Sheppards shared. No, it'd taken a good dose of blackmail to get Brady to start working at the winery.

Seemed his mother didn't have a corner on that market after all.

But Brady's situation had been different. Aidan hadn't been trying to get him on board for his own personal agenda or to fulfill his father's greatest wish. He'd done it for his brother.

Brady had been lost. Floundering. Drinking too much and being a complete ass—nothing new, really. But he hadn't even wanted anything to do with his own kid after getting J.C. pregnant. Of course, J.C. being the sister of Brady's ex-fiancée had complicated matters.

As did Brady continuing to hold on to feelings for his ex.

So when he'd pitched the idea of J.C. selling her homemade chocolates at the Diamond Dust's gift shop, Aidan had agreed—on the condition that Brady came to work for him.

His motivation was totally different from Diane's when it came to Matt. To all of them.

Leaning against the wide, center island, he crossed his feet at the ankles. "Have you considered what this is going to do to your relationship with Matt?"

Diane frowned at him. "You don't agree with what I'm doing."

"No. I don't." He didn't *agree* with her taking away his control. With her changing everything without getting his opinion first. Without asking him what he wanted.

For the first time in his life, he could sympathize with his youngest brother.

"I just hope you're willing to accept any fallout this decision might have," he continued.

Diane refilled Lily's water dish then slowly faced him. "Do you really think he'll hold this against me?"

Aidan narrowed his eyes at her. Had he detected a nervousness in his mother's voice? No sooner had the thought entered his mind than he brushed it aside. His mother didn't get nervous.

"You're asking him to give up a lot. Think about it. Brady has nothing to lose and everything to gain by this. But Matt?" He shook his head. "You and I both know he has what it takes to become one of the top names in the wine industry. And now he has to give up everything he's ever wanted to save Dad's company? To be honest, Mom, what you're doing is pretty shitty."

Her throat worked as she swallowed. "Desperate times and all that."

But though her words were said lightly, her voice wobbled. Just a bit. Enough for Aidan to realize this hadn't been an easy decision for her. "Desperate how?" he asked. "I don't see why it's so black or white... Why is it Matt or none of us? Surely there are other options."

But just like she didn't get nervous, Diane Sheppard also didn't back away from something just because it was difficult. Like him, she ran toward those situations, ready to prove herself more than capable of handling everything on her own.

He just hoped that she hadn't sacrificed her relationship with her youngest son.

"You've mentioned how this will affect Brady and Matt," she said, ignoring his blunt questions. "But what about you?"

"I have nothing to lose."

He'd already given it all up.

Reaching down, he rubbed Lily's head when she nudged his thigh. "You should know what you're getting into by asking Matt to come on board. We've always done things a certain way here—Dad's way. But that might not be good enough for Matt. He's not going to be happy running a small operation. You know his motto has always been Bigger Is Better."

She waved his words away. "Oh, I'm not worried about that. I know you'll make sure anything's that done is what's best for the Diamond Dust."

He shoved his hands into his pockets, his fingers curling. And hadn't that been the story of his life? Doing what was best for the winery. Putting his father's company, and his family's wants and needs, ahead of his own.

"Right." He cleared his throat. "You know you can count on me."

To keep things running smoothly. To fix any problems that might arise—whether those problems were his fault or not.

She laid her hand on his arm. He forced his muscles to relax. He loved his mom. He really did. But there were times when he just got tired of being Mr. Fix It.

"Have I told you how much I appreciate you?" Diane gave his arm a squeeze. "I couldn't have gotten through your father's death, kept the company going…any of it really…without you."

And as quickly as it had come, his anger dissipated with his mother's sincere words. How could he be angry about fulfilling his responsibility? Taking care of his family?

He kissed her cheek. The softness of it, her floral scent, so familiar to him. "You're one of the strongest people I know. You would've gotten through just fine on your own. But I'm glad you didn't have to."

Stepping back, she sniffed and dug a tissue out of her

sleeve. Taking off her glasses, she dabbed at her eyes as the back door opened.

"Am I late?" Brady asked in his low voice as he shut the door behind him.

Aidan finished his drink. "No. We're still waiting for the man of the hour."

Lily trotted over to Brady, her tail wagging. He sat in the chair Aidan had vacated and scratched the dog's ears. "Anyone consider what's going to happen if Matt says no?"

His question hung in the air for a moment. Their mother kept her gaze on the floor, her fingers entwined.

"The way I see it," Aidan said, rinsing out the soda can and putting it in the recycling bin, "no matter what he decides, we're going to be dealing with a whole new set of headaches."

They'd have the tension of trying to run a business together or the pain of losing their father's company. In Aidan's mind, they were screwed either way.

Lily barked twice. A moment later, Matt sauntered into the room from the hallway, his too-long hair wild around his face, his jacket unzipped over a rumpled shirt. "I'm here," he said, neither his tone nor his expression giving away his thoughts. "Let's get this over with."

CHAPTER FOUR

"Does that mean you'll accept the partnership?" his mother asked in what Matt could only describe as a hopeful tone.

Teeth clenched, he sat on a high-backed stool at the island, deliberately laid his arm on the back of the one next to him in a pose of nonchalance. "That depends. What are the terms you're offering?"

She seemed taken aback. Did she really think he'd just meekly go along with whatever stipulations she set out? "The *terms*," she said, "are that you and your brothers agree to run the Diamond Dust upon my retirement, at which time I will sign over all shares of the company. Until then, the three of you will remain in Jewell, working at the winery under its current management."

Aidan grinned—an unusual and completely unnerving event. "That'd be me."

Matt was already shaking his head. "No way am I taking orders from him."

"It's not about taking orders," his mom said, sending Aidan a reproachful look. His grin only widened. "Aidan has been President of the Diamond Dust for the past eight years. It's only reasonable that the structure remains the same until I step down as owner. Besides, until that happens, I'll still have final say on any and all decisions."

"And when is this retirement scheduled to take place?" Matt asked.

"July 27."

"That's the day Mom and Al are getting married," Aidan put in.

"Yeah. I knew that," Matt lied. He straightened, clasped his hands together on the cold counter. Met his mom's eyes and asked quietly, "And if I…if any of us… don't agree?"

"I've told you—"

"No. You haven't. Not straight out. I need to hear you say it."

For a moment, he wondered if she'd back down. But then she lifted her chin and he remembered that his mother was made of stronger stuff than that. Strong enough to risk alienating one of her own sons just to make her deceased husband's dream come true.

"If any of you don't wish to be a part of the Diamond Dust," she said, her voice steady, "then I will sell the company, the property and this house to Lester Caldwell."

Sliding to his feet, Matt looked at his brothers. Aidan stood in front of the large windows of the breakfast nook, the setting sun casting his profile in shadow. Brady sat, one hand flat on the table, the other on Lily's head.

"Is this what you both want?" Matt asked them.

Brady studied him with his cool, hooded gaze. "Does it matter?"

He cleared his throat. "Yeah," he admitted, not sure who he'd surprised more, his brothers or himself. "Yeah, it does."

Instead of answering, Aidan crossed to the island, pulled the contract from the envelope and, after flipping a few pages, signed his name with a flourish. He then handed the contract to Brady, who signed, as well.

Looked like he had his answer.

Son of a bitch.

His mother picked up the contract and pen and set them in front of Matt. "It's your decision."

"A decision indicates someone has a choice," he said coolly.

She inclined her head in agreement. "Someday, when you have children of your own, you'll understand."

"And if I don't?"

"That's a risk I'm willing to take in order to do what I think is best."

He picked up the pen. Twirled it in his hand. "There are going to be two conditions," he said, "before I agree to anything. First one," he continued when she opened her mouth as if to speak, "we give this…thing…a trial period."

Silence. Aidan and Brady exchanged a loaded glance before Aidan asked, "How long did you have in mind?"

"A year," he said, panic sliding up his spine at the thought of being stuck in Jewell for that long. "The second condition is if, at the end of that time, any of us are unhappy with the situation, we're out. No questions asked. No recriminations. Anyone who still wants in gets to keep the Diamond Dust."

"And if I don't agree?" his mother asked.

"I walk."

She didn't so much as blink. Maybe he and his brothers hadn't gotten their stubbornness from their father after all. "You'll agree to live here, to work at the Diamond Dust, for the entire year? No taking other jobs. No impromptu trips?"

Matt ground his back teeth so hard he was surprised he didn't exhale dust. "Agreed."

His mother slid the contract closer to him. "Then it's a deal."

He slid it back. Handed her the pen. "I want it in writing."

"Why, Matthew..." She laid a hand over her heart. "Don't you trust your own mother?"

"In writing."

She sighed and made a notation on the last page of the contract, adding her initials. "Your turn."

He took the pen, pressed the tip to paper. His skin grew clammy. Damn it. Damn it! None of this was what he wanted. What he'd planned for his life. Everything he'd worked for, all the long hours he'd put in to grow his reputation, to get bigger and better jobs with bigger and better wineries...it was all for nothing.

He was right back where he started.

Before he could change his mind, he scribbled his signature on the line. And effectively signed away his freedom.

OVER TWO HOURS LATER, Matt turned off the ignition of the Diamond Dust's pickup and stared across the street at Connie's small house. The porch light was off, but her ancient minivan sat in the driveway, so he figured she was home. He dug his cell phone out of his front pocket and turned it end over end in his hand.

He'd tossed the pen aside after signing the contract and walked out of his mother's kitchen without a word. There was no way he could've stayed there another second, not when it felt as if a vise was squeezing his chest, cutting off all of his air. He'd ended up at The County Line bar, a beer in front of him, a leggy blonde at his elbow trying to chat him up. But with his thoughts racing, resentment and anger flowing through him, he hadn't been able to appreciate the cold drink. Or the blonde's flirting.

He was stuck in Jewell, at least for a year. And he realized that he needed to step up and make the most of the situation at the Diamond Dust. If he wanted to resume his career in twelve months and to maintain his reputation as a world-class vintner, then he had to do what he would at any other winery.

He needed to take control.

Starting now. He exhaled heavily and pushed the button for Joan's office at Queen's Valley. After a few moments, the overseas connection went through. On the fourth ring, she barked out a "Hello."

"It's Matt," he said without preamble. "We have a problem."

"I don't like the sound of that," she said, and he could imagine her scowling as she leaned her considerable girth back in her chair. "What is it?"

"I have a…family emergency." He leaned his head back against the seat and shut his eyes. "I'm not coming back to Queen's Valley at the end of the week."

"Oh, I'm sorry. Has someone passed on, then?"

"No. Nothing like that." He cleared his throat. "The fact is, I won't be back at all."

There was a beat of heavy silence broken only by slight static on the phone. "You'd best be pulling my leg," Joan finally said.

"I'm not." He switched the phone to his other ear. "Look, I'm sorry but—"

"Fat lot of good that does me," she snapped, her voice rising. "Especially when I'm days away from harvest!"

Wincing, he held the phone away from his ear as her voice grew to a shout. "I realize this is far from ideal, but I can give you a list of names of other winemakers who might be available."

"Now, I'm sure you don't need me to tell you what you can do with your list of names, do you? We have an agreement. One I expect you to abide by."

"I can't."

"Then the next time you hear from me, it'll be through my attorney."

And the connection was cut.

He rubbed the back of his neck. That had gone about as well as he'd expected.

Climbing out of the car, he pocketed his phone and his keys and crossed the dark street. He knocked on the front door. It opened a moment later to reveal one of Connie's daughters.

"Well, hey, there," he said, surprised to find himself wanting to grin. He searched his brain for the kid's name. Anna? Amy? Damn it, he knew it started with an *A*. Or maybe it was an *E?* "Don't you look pretty."

She blinked up at him owlishly, her brown hair sticking out all over her head in about a dozen small ponytails. She wore a ruffled pink dress that was about four sizes too big and had on bright blue eye shadow and dark red lipstick that hadn't quite managed to stay on her lips.

When she just stared up at him, one hand clutching the door handle, he cleared the laughter from his throat and crouched down so they were eye to eye. She took a hesitant step back.

"You remember me, don't you?"

She nodded.

"I don't suppose you have any more of those cinnamon rolls?"

She shook her head.

After he'd woken up from his restless nap on the sofa in Aidan's office later that morning, he'd gone downstairs for some coffee and had lucked out by stepping into the kitchen just as his mom and Connie's kids were icing cinnamon rolls.

Still crouching, he shifted his weight then gave the little girl his most charming grin. Hey, it worked on females over the age of twenty-one. Might as well see if it caused a reaction in the younger set.

It didn't.

"Is your mom home?"

The little girl nodded again. Then shut the door in his face. Scratching his head, Matt straightened. A light breeze ruffled his hair and he shoved his hands into his coat pockets. He studied the quiet street. He hadn't been to this part of town since high school but it still looked the same. Houses were painted different colors, additions added, yards landscaped. But the feel of the neighborhood was the same as anywhere else in Jewell. Middle class. Well maintained. Comfortable.

He rubbed his itching palm down the front of his jeans. How the hell was he supposed to live here for an entire year? Sure, it was fine for people like Connie and Brady—even Aidan seemed to have easily readjusted.

But if working with Aidan didn't kill Matt, the boredom and suffocation of small town living surely would.

Before he could knock on the door to remind the kid he was still out there waiting, it opened. "Hi," Payton—at least he remembered one of their names—said. "You've never been to our house before."

True. While he and Connie often saw each other during his trips home, their short visits always occurred at the Diamond Dust. And away from her kids. Not that he didn't like kids. They were just so…time-consuming.

Payton was dressed as oddly as her sister, complete with matching hairstyle and makeup, but instead of a dress, she wore zebra leggings, a hot-pink fringed top and a yellow feather stole.

He had to admit they were cute as hell. "I need to talk to your mom. Can you get her for me?"

"Sure. You can come in."

Matt stepped inside a narrow living room with a large sofa to his right, a rocking chair in the corner and a TV against the opposite wall. The house wasn't what he would've expected from Connie. Sure it was clean, even though the floor was littered with toys. But the carpet was worn and the flower-print sofa had seen better days. He knew the Diamond Dust was successful—and about to become even more so once he got his hands on how things were run—just as he knew his family was more than generous with their employees.

Guess Connie chose to spend her money on other things. Like her kids. Or maybe she was one of those people who saved for the proverbial rainy day. Someone who was so focused on the future and what could go wrong, they didn't take the time to enjoy the present.

"You going to a costume party or something?" he asked Payton.

Laughing, she shut the door. "No, silly. We're playing."

She was dressed like a mini drag queen and he was

silly? Females. Even before they hit puberty they made no sense.

Payton took his hand and pulled him to the other side of the room. He stumbled over a plastic box before catching his balance.

"You can sit here." She pointed to a wooden rocking chair currently occupied by a naked Barbie doll.

Picking up the doll by its feet—the only respectful place he could think of—he stood there, feeling way more awkward than he'd ever felt when he'd had his hands on a real-live naked woman. "Is this yours?" he asked Payton.

She shook her head and, as gracefully as a ballerina, leaped over a small pile of boxed puzzles. "She's Abby's."

Abby. At least he'd been close. He held the Barbie out to the younger girl. "You'd better put some clothes on her. I'd hate for her to be arrested for indecent exposure."

Abby's eyes widened and, to his horror, filled with tears. Shit.

"I was kidding," he said, not caring that he sounded almost as panicked as the kid looked. The last thing he needed tonight was a bawling kid. "Honest. Barbie can stay naked for as long as she likes. I'm sure Ken won't mind, either."

He held the doll out to her and she darted behind her sister, who had come back with a DVD in one hand, an iPod in the other. Fumbling a bit with the iPod, Payton grabbed Barbie and gave it to Abby.

"Do you like movies?" Payton asked, holding up the DVD. "This is *High School Musical 3,* and this—" she raised her other hand "—is the iPod my Daddy got me. He—"

"Did you girls clean up like I asked?" Connie's voice came from the stairway to Matt's right. A moment later she appeared at the top of the stairs carrying a full laundry basket.

"Hey," he said, stepping over to take it from her, "let me help you with that."

She frowned as he took the laundry and, after a moment's debate, set the basket on the sofa since he couldn't find room on the floor.

"Matt. What are you doing…" She shook her head. "You know what? Hold that thought." Eyes narrowing, she faced the girls, hands on her hips. "What is the rule about opening the door to strangers?"

"We're not supposed to," Payton said in a monotone, as if reciting something that'd been drilled into her head a hundred times. Abby, sucking her thumb, sidled over to her sister. "We're supposed to get you right away."

"And yet, I come upstairs and there's a strange man in our house."

"That hurts," Matt said with faux cheerfulness. "Especially since I've known you half my life."

No one even looked at him. "See? He knows us, Mommy," Payton said. "Plus, Diane's his mom and Aidan's his brother."

"Yes," Connie said, "but my point is that you couldn't

have known who was at the door without opening it first. Therefore, you broke the rule."

"Nuh-uh. I knew who was there because Abby told me."

Connie raised her eyes as if beseeching the heavens, and Matt ducked his head to hide his grin. Payton was a girl after his own heart, tossing her sister into the fire that way to save her own hide. There'd been many times he'd done the same to his brothers.

Connie turned her attention to the sprite standing behind Payton. "Is that true, Abby?"

"I wooked out the window fuwst," she said softly, speaking around her thumb.

"That window?" Connie pointed to the window behind a fat, brown armchair. "And don't you dare answer me with that thumb in your mouth."

Abby slowly lowered her hand. "The window in the door."

Matt followed Connie's gaze to the half-circle window at the top of the door. The one that you'd have to be at least six feet tall to look out of.

"But how did you see…?" Connie held up her hands. "No. Don't tell me. I'll sleep better tonight not knowing."

"That's probably wise," Matt murmured.

Connie rubbed her temples. This was why he had no desire to have kids. Seemed to him that while they were cute and could be amusing at times, they weren't worth the headaches they caused. God knew, he and his brothers had given their mother more than her fair share.

"I'm not going to punish you this time but I don't want either one of you opening the door when I'm not up here. And just to make it perfectly clear, that means that you are not to open the door under any circumstances unless I'm standing in this room. Is that understood?" Both girls nodded. "Good. Now go on up and wash your faces and get on your pajamas."

Holding hands, the girls raced past him and out of the room. "It's partly my fault," Matt said. "I should've waited on the porch while they got you."

"They still should've known better," she said with a shrug before bending down to swipe up the forgotten Barbie along with a handful of miniature doll clothes. "So, what's up?"

"Would you believe I was in the neighborhood?" he asked easily, once again trying out his most charming grin.

And once again, it had no effect. Must be the Henkel females were immune.

"Well, since I've never once before seen you in the neighborhood... No," she said. "I wouldn't believe it."

I wouldn't believe you. She hadn't spoken those words but the implication was clear. Fair enough. He didn't need her to do anything other than listen to him. "Actually, I dropped by because I want to talk to you about the vineyards."

CONNIE DIDN'T KNOW WHICH surprised her most. That Matt was in her living room, big as life and gorgeous to boot, looking as out of place with his shaggy brown hair and expensive clothes as the Queen of England would look chowing down a corn dog at a convenience store. Or that he was there to discuss her vineyards.

Or that he somehow seemed…different than usual. Oh, sure, he was smiling at her, his arms relaxed at his sides, but his smile didn't reach his green eyes. And there seemed to be an edge to him that she'd never seen before.

"Did something happen?" she asked, her mind automatically running through scenarios. Fire. Flood. Vandals taking axes to the vines. None of which were even close to being likely.

"No. That's part of the problem."

She rolled her eyes. "And that makes no sense."

"You're late with the pruning," he said in a mild tone normal people would use to discuss the weather. Not to accuse someone of not knowing their own job. "If you wait too long to prune, you'll negatively affect crop size."

She gaped at him, her hands tightening around Barbie, the sharp plastic of the doll's hands digging into her skin. "Excuse me?"

He looked at her as if she and Barbie shared a brain—and Barbie was currently in possession of it. "I said, you're late—"

"No," she said, throwing Barbie and her clothes into a pink, plastic bin and snapping the lid shut. "Not *excuse me could you repeat yourself? Excuse me* as in *where do you get off telling me how to do my job?*"

"It's my job, too. And besides, I'm right."

She brushed away his words with a wave of her hand. "Just because we're in the same field, doesn't give you the right to impose your opinions on me." No one told her how to run her vineyards. "Do I ever show up at your home—unannounced, I might add—and insinuate you don't know what you're doing?"

"Of course not," he said, his grin widening, becoming cocky—as if he found it amusing that she thought, even for a moment, that she knew half as much about viticulture as he did.

It took all her willpower not to knock him upside his too-good-looking, arrogant head.

Just because he'd gained his knowledge at a university while she was taught hers out in the field didn't mean he knew more than she did. Didn't mean he was better than her.

"Late pruning only affects crop size when you prune after bud break," she told him, proud of how calm, how rational she sounded. "And for your information, I'm not late with anything. Blocks one through three are already pruned."

"So the Chardonnay's done," he said, surprising her that he remembered which grapes were growing in that section of the vineyard. "What's on the schedule for tomorrow?"

"Okay, I give up." She picked up the puzzles and set them on one of the shelves by the television. "What's going on? Why are you suddenly taking an interest in the Diamond Dust?"

He scratched his cheek. "I take it you haven't spoken with Aidan or my mom tonight?"

"Not since I left work."

"So you haven't heard about Mom's big plan to get me to be a part of the winery?"

Scooping up a pile of dress-up clothes from the floor, she froze. Her hands tingled, felt stiff. Cold. She shoved the clothes into the wooden toy box in the corner before facing him. "What plan?"

A muscle worked in his jaw as if he was grinding his teeth. But when he spoke, his voice was mild, the hint of Southern in his words thicker than usual. "Mom threatened to sell the Diamond Dust if Aidan, Brady and I don't agree to run it. Together." Shoulders slouched, he smirked, making him look like the rebellious teen he'd once been. "Just like Dad always wanted."

CHAPTER FIVE

CONNIE SHOOK HER HEAD but the buzzing in her ears continued as she gaped at him.

"You okay?" Matt asked, reaching out as if to steady her.

She stepped back. "When...why..."

"You really didn't know about any of this?"

"No." With her breath locked in her chest, he probably couldn't hear her. "No," she repeated louder, hoping he didn't notice the way her voice trembled.

But suddenly, the tension between Diane and Aidan these past few weeks made sense. And here Connie thought she'd imagined the sudden silence whenever she entered a room where the two of them were in conversation.

Diane wanted her sons to run the Diamond Dust. She'd offered a partnership to Matt.

Connie's partnership.

Her throat tightened. "Diane would sell the winery?"

"So she says."

"We both know your mother doesn't say anything she doesn't mean." Connie felt numb. She pushed a hand through her hair and tugged at the ends. "So... did you?"

She held her breath. But no matter what his answer, her future would be irrevocably changed.

"Did I agree?" he asked. She nodded. "On the dotted line," he said with a sharp grin that held more bitterness than joy.

"Is that why you're here, questioning how I do things? You think you have the right since you're my new..." She pressed her lips together. Nope. She couldn't do it. She couldn't call this charming, irresponsible man her boss. Not when he'd never given the Diamond Dust, or his own family, a second thought. "Because you're now a partner in the winery?"

He picked up a plastic dog—one of the Barbie doll's pets—and flipped it from one hand to the other. Back and forth. Back and forth. "Actually, it's not quite that straightforward."

And all that flipping was driving her insane. She snatched the toy from him and, doing what she did when she wanted to set something out of her daughters' reach, placed it on the top shelf of her bookcase. "Why don't you try to explain it to me. Use small words and maybe I'll be able to follow along."

"The partnership doesn't go into effect until Mom retires in July." Seeming lost without something to do with his hands, he tucked them in his jacket pockets. But though he stood still, there was a barely concealed energy about him. An intensity she'd never seen in him before. "Until then, we're all to work together—under President Aidan, of course."

Some of the tightness in her chest eased. He wasn't a partner. Things hadn't changed. Yet. "And you thought the best way to work with me would be to stop by, tell me what to do and insult how I run things?"

He smiled, slow and easy. "Now, there's no need to get defensive. We're all on the same side here."

"Are we?" Seemed to her, they were on two very different sides. She wanted to preserve her job and her place at the Diamond Dust. And he wanted...well...she wasn't sure what exactly. But she was going to find out. She closed the distance between them until she was close enough to smell his cologne, something spicy and undoubtedly expensive. "Want to know what I think?"

His gaze narrowed slightly, dropped to her mouth for one long second before returning to her eyes. "I can hardly wait."

A tingle of awareness slid up her spine as real and as unwelcome as the heat filling her cheeks. Okay, so he was tall and broad-shouldered and sexy as hell with his shaggy, too-long hair, sharp jaw and those mesmerizing green eyes. And yes, it had been a really long time since a man had looked at her with such intensity. Interest.

If that interest was even real. With someone like Matt, who was used to twisting situations to his advantage, it was hard to tell.

Ignoring the way her stomach pitched, she patted his cheek, the roughness of his whiskers scratching her palm. "I think you came over here believing if you batted your eyes at me and gave me one of those heart-stopping grins of yours, that I'd melt at your feet."

Though he stiffened, she kept her hand on his face. His expression never changed. "Does my grin make your heart stop?"

She curled her fingers and lowered her arm before she gave in to the urge to put a little sting behind her tap. "I'm not some young, empty-headed coed. I'm not going to fall at your feet just because you throw some of your two-bit, canned charm my way. Sorry, buddy, not going to work."

Something hot and real and almost dangerous flashed across his face. But before she could do more than blink in surprise, it was gone.

"Sugar," he said in a low voice, "there is nothing two-bit about me. And if I wanted to charm you, you can bet your sweet ass you'd be charmed. Now, the only reason I'm here is because I want to discuss the vineyards and your style of managing them."

"I run things the way your father taught me. There. Discussion over."

"What is your problem?" he asked, confusion warring with irritation in his eyes.

Okay, so he really was clueless. About so many things—mainly that he'd been offered everything she'd ever wanted. And how unfair was that? He'd left the Diamond Dust and his family without so much as a backward glance while she was the one who'd stood by them, who'd supported them. Loved them.

Her mother had warned her. She'd often felt threatened

by her only child's relationship with the Sheppards. Envious of the time Connie spent with Diane. Blood is thicker than water, Margaret Dexter would often say. Families take care of their own first.

Who would've ever guessed her mother could be right?

"My problem," she said, "is you think that just because you went away to school, just because you're the almighty Matt Sheppard, vintner extraordinaire, you can waltz in here and tell me how to run my vineyards. The last thing I'm going to do is stand here and let you question my competency. Not when I have two little girls to put to bed, a mountain of laundry to sort, fold and put away, and a sink full of dirty dishes needing my attention."

"I didn't mean to interrupt your night," he said stiffly, his cool, uptight tone reminding her of Aidan when he got his back up.

"I'm sure you weren't thinking of anything other than what you wanted and how to get it." As usual. Taking hold of his arm, she tugged him across the room. His muscles flexed under her fingers, his body heat seeped through his sleeve and into her skin.

"My only concern was for the Diamond Dust," he said, sounding so sincere, she would've believed him had he not spent the past ten years ignoring the winery and his family. "I'd have thought you, of all people, would understand that."

"Am I supposed to know what you mean by that?" she asked as she opened the door.

"Just that you've been with the winery a long time. Don't you want what's best for it?"

She trembled. With anger. With the unfairness of it all. Because of course she wanted what was best for the business. Hadn't she proven that with her years of loyalty and hard work? And to have him, of all people, question that dedication?

It was too much.

Using both hands, she shoved at his chest, pushing him over the threshold onto the porch.

"Hey," he said, scowling as he regained his balance. "No need to get violent."

"The next time you want to discuss business with me on my personal time, call first. In the meantime, you're not a full partner in the Diamond Dust yet, therefore you're not my boss. When that changes, we'll talk about how I do my job. During work hours and at my office at the winery."

Then she had the distinct and, she had to admit, immense pleasure of shutting the door on Matt Sheppard's handsome face.

"Is it true?"

At the sound of Connie's curt question, Aidan shared a look with Pam Campbell, the gift shop manager. From her place on the floor, Lily raised her head, her tail wagging. But when she saw Payton and Abby weren't with Connie, she lay down and closed her eyes again.

"You'll have to be more specific," Aidan said, still looking over the inventory sheet Pam had just handed him. "My mind reading abilities don't work this early in the morning."

Connie didn't move from the office doorway. The morning sunlight streamed through the window, illuminating her thin frame. "Did your mom threaten to sell the Diamond Dust?"

Pam gasped and whirled around to stare at Connie. Aidan shut his eyes. Damn it. This was exactly why he and his mother had decided not to share her ultimatum with their employees. The last thing they'd wanted was for people to unnecessarily worry about their jobs.

"No one's selling the winery," Aidan said, meeting Connie's, then Pam's eyes. "Everything's fine."

Neither of them looked as if they believed his lie. Oh, the winery was safe. But even Aidan couldn't swallow the line that everything was fine. Not when he'd be working with his youngest brother full-time.

Connie cocked one hip and crossed her arms. "If it's not true, then why did your brother show up at my house last night and tell me she'd threatened to do just that?"

"Brady went to your house?"

"Not Brady," Connie said. "Matt."

And the way she spit out his youngest brother's name made it all too clear what had happened. Matt had messed things up. No surprise there.

But he hadn't expected Matt to tell people about their little...problem. He'd figured his brother would sulk for a few days, maybe hide out and lick his wounds. Or, more than likely, hole up somewhere and try to come up with a way out of the contract he'd signed. A way to run away.

Aidan handed the inventory sheet back to Pam. "I'll stop by the gift shop sometime this afternoon to finish going over these."

She hesitated, obviously not thrilled at being dismissed before she'd gotten more information. But, the older woman was efficient, quiet and more than willing to wait out the storm. She slowly got to her feet and glanced back at Connie.

Connie nodded at Pam. "I'll fill you in once I've gotten the full story. Someone around here has to be responsible for letting people know what's really going on."

Aidan pinched the bridge of his nose. "That's not helping." He looked at Pam as he sat back in his chair. "But Connie's right. You know as soon as she's done here she'll tell you everything and then you, in turn, can tell Kathleen, Janice, Lisa and Leslie," he said, referring to the four women who worked under Pam at the gift shop.

By the end of the day everyone at the Diamond Dust, employees and customers alike, along with half of Jewell, would know Sheppard family business. How their mother had to resort to blackmail to get her three sons to work together.

One of the consequences of running a small business in his hometown. Nothing was secret or sacred.

"All right," Pam said. "I'll talk to you later then."

And though she was looking his way, he didn't doubt she was speaking to Connie.

Once he and Connie were alone, Aidan got up and walked around to sit on the front of his desk, Lily padding along next to him. "I'd appreciate it if you wouldn't try to induce panic in my employees," he said dryly.

"Oh, please. It could be raining meteors and Pam wouldn't bat an eye. The only time I've seen her even remotely worked up was during that Spring Fling Tasting Event when Pastor Rice had a few too many tastings and got sick all over the patio. And even then not one hair came loose from that braid she insists on wearing."

"If only all of my employees were as calm under pressure."

"Hey, I'm a rock under pressure. I just don't like surprises, that's all." She shut the door behind her and entered the room, her walk more of a swagger than a stride. One that clearly told him she was ready to do battle. She stopped in front of him. "Why didn't you tell me?"

That's when he saw that despite her trademark smirk and the steel in her voice, hurt lingered in her eyes.

His fingers curled into his palms. Damn. Now he had to not only reassure her that her job was safe but soothe any hurt feelings, as well.

Some days he really hated being the boss.

"I didn't tell you because it didn't seem necessary. It's…family business."

For a moment, she didn't move. Didn't so much as blink. He wondered if she was even breathing. But then she inhaled shakily. "So you and your brothers really are going to take over the Diamond Dust?"

"I contacted our attorney first thing this morning to get started on the paperwork to transfer the business from Mom's hands to ours."

Connie paled but recovered quickly. "What's Matt's job?"

He frowned. "Excuse me?"

"Matt's job, his position at the winery. He mentioned he'll be working here until the partnership goes through, and then last night he shows up at my house and starts accusing me of not pruning early enough. Questioning me about how I run the vineyard. So now I can't help but wonder if…" She swallowed. "I need to know if my position here is secure."

He rose to his feet. Damn it, what had Matt said to her? "Of course."

Instead of seeming relieved, Connie looked as if he'd just reached out and slapped her. "Is he taking over the vineyards?"

"Taking over? No." He paused. He and Diane had planned on telling Connie all of this later today but there was no way to avoid it now. "You two will be working together. Co-managers, you could say."

"Co-managers," she repeated tonelessly. She nodded once, hooking her thumbs through the front belt loops on her jeans. "I see. So I'm not fired. Just demoted."

He drummed his fingers on the desk, which had Lily whining. "No one is demoting you. You'll still have the same pay. The same responsibilities."

"Just not the same authority."

"The same everything."

"Really? So what happens if my new co-manager and I have a difference of opinion on how something should be done or about who should handle a certain task? Oh, I know, we could play Rock, Paper, Scissors. Winner gets to be in charge for the day."

"If you and Matt have a difference of opinion," he said tightly, "you'll sit down and hash it out and do what's best for the winery." He stepped over his dog and walked back behind his desk. "Give him a chance. He's good at what he does. One of the best."

"Of course he is." She sounded so resigned, so sad, Aidan racked his brain trying to figure out what he'd said to hurt her. "He's a Sheppard."

"What's that supposed to mean?" he asked.

She shook her head. "I need to get going. Wouldn't want to be late the first day with my new co-manager." She turned on her heel and walked away.

What the hell had that been about? He blew out a heavy breath then sat in his chair and leaned his head back, staring up at the ceiling.

He liked this situation less than Connie did. And while he'd wanted his brothers to be a part of the winery for years, he hadn't truly believed the day would ever come when the three of them would work together. But now, in addition to running his father's company, he'd have to babysit Matt.

Not that he minded being equal partners, shut out of his position as head of the company after giving up everything for the Diamond Dust.

No. He didn't mind at all.

His entire life, Aidan knew more was expected of him. Maybe that was because he was the oldest child or because of his own controlled personality. It didn't matter which. The end result was the same. Everything, from the straight A's he'd received to his good behavior, had been done as an example to his brothers. To please his parents. To do what was right.

So when his father became sick, Aidan had returned to Jewell to take over the Diamond Dust.

He never regretted it.

He couldn't. Because if he did, that would mean he'd wasted the past eight years of his life, had set aside his own dreams and goals and career aspirations for nothing.

If he did, it'd mean he'd lost his wife for no reason.

He took his responsibilities to the winery and his family seriously. It was up to him to make sure everything ran smoothly. To set his brothers straight when they messed up. To make sure things went the way they should. According to his plans.

As the boss, he got to deal with the good and the bad. Unhappy employees. Bad weather. Rising insecticide prices. Taxes and laws and all the other headaches a small business owner dealt with.

And he was damned good at it.

Even though sometimes he wished he wasn't. Even

if there were times he wished he could be more like Matt. Wished he could leave Jewell and the Diamond Dust and never look back.

"I NEED TO TALK TO YOU."

Matt glanced at Aidan as he walked down the row of Viognier grapes Matt was pruning along with Keith Waddle and Tony Aitken, two of the three full-time vineyard workers.

"You want to talk? Start cutting. Unless you've spent so much time on your ass behind that big desk you've forgotten how to handle a pair of pruning shears."

Keith and Tony laughed, their movements never slowing as they worked, snipping off branches and tossing them into the middle of the row to be chopped up and used as compost.

Without a word Aidan took the shears from Matt's gloved hand. Matt smirked but it soon faded as Aidan quickly, effortlessly and professionally pruned two vines in the time it would take Matt to get through a vine and a half.

He held out the shears to Matt. "I'll always be faster than you."

Matt took the shears, slid them into his back pocket by the handles. "I'll always be better looking. And taller."

When Aidan inclined his head then started walking, Matt fell into step beside his brother as they went back toward the gift shop and winery buildings. The morning was cool and clear, and the frost-covered grass crunched under their feet. "Whatever it is you want to discuss must be important," Matt said. "It dragged you away from your office and got you to hike all the way out here. Why didn't you take one of the trucks?"

"I like to walk," Aidan said simply, the morning breeze ruffling his short hair. "And it is important. I know it might be a stretch for you, but could you try not to piss off our employees? Maybe you should take a management course or two at the community college. Might help you learn how to deal with people."

Matt tugged his knit hat lower over his ears. "I take it you spoke with Connie."

Aidan paused at the end of the row. "Mom and I were going to meet with her later today to discuss the changes happening here. Instead, Connie shows up at my office first thing this morning, demanding to know what's going on. What were you thinking? Why the hell did you go to her house last night?"

A mole darted out from beneath a small pile of leaves. Matt stomped his booted foot in front of it to get it to scurry off in the other direction. "I was out," he said, feeling as defensive and uncomfortable as he had when he'd been sixteen and tried to explain to his parents how an empty condom wrapper had been left in their car. The car that he'd borrowed the night before. As for what he'd been thinking last night, that was easy. He'd been thinking he'd been royally screwed over by his own family and had wanted to do something, anything to try and salvage his career and his plans for the future. Had wanted to show he wouldn't sit around waiting for

Aidan to tell him what to do, when to do it. He was taking charge.

He picked up a pencil-thin cane that had been pruned from the vine and tapped it against his thigh. "I don't see what the problem is. I had a few questions about the vineyard and decided to see if Connie could answer them for me."

"The problem is that in a few months you're going to own the Diamond Dust." Aidan straightened the heavy tag with the row number and grape type that was hanging on the thick end post. "You have to start thinking about what's best for the company, and that includes what's best for the people who work for you. Which means you can't go around upsetting your employees and making them think their jobs are in jeopardy."

"I never said anything about her job being in jeopardy." Maybe he had questioned how she did that job, but only because he'd been forced into this whole rotten situation. "She jumped to conclusions. Are you sure she's not..."

Aidan raised one eyebrow. "Not what?"

"Not like her mother?"

Everyone knew Margaret Dexter suffered from mental illness. Maybe her daughter took after her.

"You're an idiot," Aidan said flatly.

Matt held up his hands. "Hey, no need to resort to name-calling. I just think I'm entitled to know if someone I'll be working very closely with has any... issues."

Aidan pinched the bridge of his nose. "Connie's been

with us for over fifteen years. She's loyal, hardworking and loves the Diamond Dust. If you want your working relationship with her to go smoothly, why don't you try some of that dubious charm you claim to have? Try listening to her, working with her instead of proving you know more."

I'm not going to fall at your feet just because you throw some of your two-bit, canned charm my way.

The back of his neck heated. No way would he admit he'd tried that already and been called out on it. Instead he gave his brother an easy grin. "Sage advice. I'll take it under consideration."

Aidan's mouth flattened—just like their father's used to when Matt gave him a flippant response. "See that you do."

He turned to leave.

"Why'd you agree to this?" Matt asked before his brother could walk away. "You don't want this any more than I do."

Matt could see Aidan's shoulders stiffen, but when he slowly faced him, his eyes were cool. His expression clear. "I've spent the past eight years of my life keeping the winery going. Do you really think I could just walk away now?"

"Even if it means working with me?"

Something flashed in his brother's eyes but was gone too quickly for Matt to decipher it. "Even then."

Matt sneered, told himself the prickling sensation between his shoulder blades was anger. "Always willing to take one for the team, aren't you? Just like Dad taught you."

Aidan stepped closer but Matt didn't budge an inch, just straightened to his full height. He'd long ago stopped giving ground to anyone.

"Dad taught me a lot of things," Aidan said quietly. "How important it is to keep one's word. That a handshake is as good as a written promise. And that a man's first loyalty should be to his family. Lessons he taught you, as well. The difference between us is that I chose to learn a thing or two while you continually choose not to."

That wasn't the only difference between them, Matt thought as Aidan walked away. Damn it, he wasn't going to feel guilty about the choices he'd made. Aidan had given up his plans to become an attorney to keep their father's company going. No one had held a gun to his head and forced him to return.

Not the way Matt was being forced.

He whirled on his heel and began walking back to where he'd left Keith and Tony. Aidan got off on playing the savior.

A man's first loyalty should be to his family.

Holding his gloves in one hand, he smacked them across a post. Damn it. He was here, wasn't he? He'd given up his position at Queen's Valley to save his father's company. To help his brothers get what they wanted.

He picked up his pace. His blood heated. Twigs snapped under his feet.

He'd shown family loyalty and lost his future. Now he was going to go back to looking out for himself.

CHAPTER SIX

IT'S FAMILY BUSINESS.

Guess she now knew where she stood, Connie thought later that afternoon, Aidan's words still rang in her ears, competing with Carrie Underwood's "Undo It" on her iPod. Diane had come up with a blackmail scheme to get her sons to work together, and none of the Sheppards had thought enough of their employees to tell them the truth.

They hadn't thought enough of her.

While Carrie sang about some rotten bastard making her cry, Connie viciously snipped off a piece of one-year-old Pinot Noir wood with her pruning shears before yanking it free of the trellis wire and tossing it aside. The Pinot Noir had been trained to a cordon—two arms of the plant extended on either side of the trunk along the first trellis wire. Out of those cordons grew thick extensions, and out of those extensions the one-year-old wood grew—shoots a couple feet long, the thickest ones no larger in diameter than her pinkie.

It was a gorgeous day to spend in the vineyard. The sky was a clear, brilliant blue; the bright sun and the physical nature of her work warmed her enough that she'd hung her heavy jacket on one of the posts fifty or so vines ago, leaving her to work in her hooded sweat-shirt and favourite ball cap. The air was crisp and just this side of cool and still held the feel of winter. But soon that would change. Spring would come, and with it her vines would grow and flourish. Renew themselves.

She just hoped she still had a job at the Diamond Dust when that happened.

She continued working, cutting off dead growth, pruning back the healthiest one-year-old wood, leaving spurs of two buds on each. But she couldn't enjoy it. Not after Matt had showed up at her house last night and oh-so-calmly dropped the bomb that everything she'd wanted was out of her reach forever.

While she was casting blame, she'd toss Diane in there for coming up with this whole ludicrous idea. And Aidan for...well, for being Aidan.

I need to know if my position here is secure.

She'd asked him that and what had he said?

Of course.

Her throat constricted. That was it. But it wasn't enough. She wanted a guarantee of her place within the winery. Assurance that he valued her as an employee, or that he and Diane wouldn't just toss her aside now that they'd gotten what they'd obviously always wanted.

Finished with the new wood, she exchanged her hand shears for a pair of loppers—what she thought of as supersize pruners with long handles. She removed old growth as well as a few old spurs that didn't have any new wood on them.

Her phone vibrated in her pocket. Tucking the loppers

under her arm, she dug it out and glanced at the number on the screen.

Her mother was calling.

She considered letting it go to voice mail. After all, she'd already spoken with her twice today: once when she'd stopped by her mom's house on the way to work and again when Margaret had called during lunch not two hours ago.

Luckily, her mother hadn't heard the news about the Sheppard boys taking over the winery. But if…when… that changed, Connie knew what Margaret would say.

I told you not to wish for things out of your reach, Constance. You always did think too highly of yourself.

Blood is thicker than water.

But no sooner had her phone stopped vibrating than it started up again. And if she didn't answer soon, her mom would give up on reaching Connie through her cell and call the office phone. Then the Sheppard house.

Her mother was un-ignorable.

She took her earbuds out and looped them loosely around her neck before answering. "Hello?"

"Constance, thank God," Margaret said, "I've been trying to get ahold of you for hours."

More like five minutes. Then again, her mother was known for…well, for many things. And while exaggerating was on that long list, it didn't come close to being in the number one spot.

"Mom." Connie's fingers tightened on her phone. From the agitation in Margaret's voice, she wasn't about to have a pleasant conversation. "Are you all right?"

"No. I need you to come here right away."

She grew queasy. "What's wrong? What is it?"

Connie's head filled with possibilities—her mother could've fallen. Or cut herself. Or Connie could arrive at the house she grew up in, only to discover Margaret lying on the floor, an empty bottle of sleeping pills by her head. The same way it had happened when Connie was eleven.

Connie's heart raced and she started hurrying down the row. "Mom? Mom what is it?"

"I'm out of milk."

Stopping, she shut her eyes and exhaled heavily. Milk. Dear God.

She rubbed at the headache brewing behind her left temple. "No problem. I'll drop some off after work."

"I need it now," Margaret said, her tone going from fragile to petulant. "Paula Deen made homemade pudding on her TV show and I want to make it but I need milk. And heavy cream."

And then the day got even worse as Connie saw Matt coming toward her, looking all sorts of sexy with his hair pulled back into a short ponytail and golden stubble covering his chin and cheeks. He held her coat in one of his large hands.

Damn. She just couldn't catch a break.

She cleared her throat. "Mom, I'm working."

"What is this world coming to if a mother can't call her only child when she needs something?"

"Of course you can call me." And did with alarming frequency. Matt grew closer, close enough to hear every word she uttered. She hunched her shoulders and turned her back to him. "As soon as I'm done for the day—"

"What would it hurt for you to take an hour off? Or won't the Sheppards let one of their employees have time off to help her own mother?"

"If it was an emergency—"

"So I have to be on death's door to get a little attention from my only child?"

"That's not—"

"Never mind," she wailed, reminding Connie of Abby when she had one of her meltdowns. And oh, please, dear God, let that be the only similarity between her mother and either of her daughters. "I realize now that your job is more important than your mother."

"You know that's not true—"

But her mother had already hung up.

It wasn't the worst conversation Connie had had with her. Her fingers trembling only slightly, she clicked her phone off then slowly turned to find Matt with his arms crossed, her coat still in his hand, his eyes on her.

"Everything okay?" he asked in his low, easy voice.

"Fine."

She picked up the pruning shears and started on the next vine. Felt him still watching her. She whirled around. "What?"

He held her coat up. "Just thought you might like your jacket back."

She snatched it from him. "You look like you have something to say."

He shrugged but his gaze remained watchful. Intense.

"Actually, I did want to discuss having the crew start earlier in the mornings. By not starting until nine, we're wasting almost two hours of sunlight."

"You talked with the crew?" she asked, her fingers tightening around the handles of the pruners. "My crew?"

"The Diamond Dust's vineyard crew. Yes. They seemed okay with the time change."

She opened her mouth to tell him he had no right discussing anything with her crew but snapped her lips together. Thanks to Diane and Aidan, Matt had every right.

While she wasn't sure what she had anymore.

Her sight blurred. She blinked rapidly, ducking her head as if concentrating on her pruning. "What time would you like us to start?"

"Seven-thirty."

Seven-thirty? If she dropped the girls off at school before eight, they had to attend the school's morning day care program. Something she'd never done before, although they did go to the afternoon session. But hey, since she no longer needed to worry about saving money to buy into the winery, she could afford to pay for another hour of child care a day.

"Great. I guess I'll see you bright and early tomorrow morning then."

He untangled a cut shoot from the vine. "Is this how it's going to be from now on?"

She studied two shoots from the same extension. Choosing the thicker one, the one closer to the cordon, she cut it off above the second bud. "I don't know what you're talking about."

"I'm talking about you working here alone when Keith, Tony and I are pruning a totally different section and Terry is using the tractor in the Chardonnay blocks."

To mow over the cut shoots to use them as ground cover and mulch. "I figured you three had the Viognier under control so I thought I'd get a head start on these."

"You're avoiding me."

Heat climbed into her cheeks but she forced herself to meet his eyes. "That, too."

He grinned. "Know what I've always liked about you?"

"My sunny disposition?"

"Your honesty."

And why that had a lump forming in her throat, she had no idea.

Her phone vibrated again. Taking a deep breath, she checked the screen, answered it immediately when she saw it was Diane. "Hello?"

"Connie, it's me. Listen, your mother just called here."

She pressed her knuckle against her forehead and hoped her head didn't simply explode.

"I'll..." She'll what? Tell Margaret to stop? As if that had ever worked before. "I'll talk to her about not calling your personal line." Again. "I'm really sorry she's bothering you."

"You have nothing to apologize for," Diane said. "Honey, she's having chest pains. She called an ambulance to take her to the E.R. because she didn't want to tear you away from your work to take her."

Connie frowned, switched the phone to her other ear. "Chest pains?" Her mother wouldn't try to manipulate her into paying attention to her by faking a heart attack. Would she? "I…I need to get to the hospital," she said, unable to stop a ball of fear from forming in her stomach.

"Of course. Take all the time you need. Why don't you call the school and tell them I'll get the girls today? You can pick them up here when you're done."

For the first time, she wanted to tell a Sheppard no. Wanted to insist that she didn't need them, any of them, after the way they'd kept things from her. Brushed her contributions to the Diamond Dust aside as if all of her hard work didn't matter.

As if she didn't matter.

But she couldn't force a confrontation out into the open. Not when she was too afraid of how it might end. "That would be great. Thanks."

She clicked off the phone and bent to gather up her tools and her jacket. When she straightened, Matt was blocking her way. "Everything okay?"

"Fine." She edged to the side to move around him but he didn't budge.

Instead, he shocked her by taking hold of her upper arm, his warm, strong fingers gripping her gently. "You sure?" he asked quietly.

Their gazes locked. Something potent…elemental passed between them. Her mouth dried. Despite her heavy sweatshirt, gooseflesh rose on her arms. She shivered.

"Hey," he said, stepping closer, raising his free hand to nudge up the rim of her ballcap. He bent his knees slightly so they were eye to eye. "What is it?"

God. She wanted nothing more than to lean into his heat and strength. To be held. Comforted.

She wanted to be the one being taken care of, if only for a moment.

She stepped back, forcing him to let go. Hugging her jacket to her chest like a shield, she licked her dry lips. "My mom's been rushed to the hospital."

"She sick?"

Yes, Margaret was sick. But not just physically. Bipolar disorder. Periods of mania, where she experienced the highest of highs for anywhere from days to weeks, followed by crushing depression.

And while she'd suffered with her disease for as long as Connie could remember, it seemed to be getting worse, either because her mother was getting older or because she was off her meds. Again.

Connie raised her head but couldn't meet Matt's eyes. "She's having chest pains." She stepped around him. "I really have to go."

"If there's anything I can do…"

But she just shook her head and walked away.

"SURELY YOU CAN CHANGE your plans," Diane said later that night as Matt got a bottle of water out of her refrigerator. "After all, we're having your favorites. Baked ziti, garlic-cheese bread, and the girls made homemade brownies for dessert."

And it all smelled damn good, too. Good enough to make his mouth water. But he wasn't going to let her sway him into spending the evening pretending they were one big happy family. That everything was okay between them. Not when he was still so angry.

He ignored how hopeful she looked. "Thanks, but I'm not hungry."

She frowned and exchanged a loaded look with Al, her tall, heavyset, silver-haired fiancé, as she handed him a stack of plates. Al, for his part, kept his expression neutral, his thoughts to himself, choosing instead to take the plates into the dining room, where Connie's kids were helping to set the table.

"But, Matthew," his mother said, "we haven't had a family dinner since you've been home. Aidan will be here, and Brady and J.C. are coming, plus Connie and the girls are staying..."

He twisted the lid off his water. Tightened it back on again. "Then you already have plenty of guests. You don't need me."

And he walked out before she could try and guilt him into changing his mind. In the foyer, he set the bottle down on the small table in front of an oval mirror. He grabbed the running shoes he'd left by the bottom of the stairway and sat on the second to bottom step.

"Where are you going?"

Startled, he raised his head. Payton stood a few feet

away wearing a pair of jeans and a purple top with a huge sparkly flower on it. "Hey, short stuff."

She set her hands on her hips. "Aren't you eating dinner with us?"

"Nope."

"Why not?"

He put his right shoe on and tied it. "Because I'm going for a run."

She studied him, her lips pursed, her eyes narrowed behind her glasses. Boy, she sure had the look of her mother.

"Okay," she said, then ran out of the foyer.

Glad someone understood his need to escape. Even if that someone was under ten. He was antsy, wound up. He needed a break. A few hours away from his family and their expectations of him.

So he'd go for a run. Push his body physically in the hopes that it'd help smooth out some of his edginess. Then he'd hit The County Line or The Empire bar for something to eat. Maybe a few drinks. Somewhere he could spend a few hours where no one wanted anything from him.

He stood and crossed to the front door.

"Wait!" Payton ran over to him, her hand held out. "Here."

She had a large, misshapen brownie in her hand. She must've squeezed it because there was a thumb-size dent in the center.

He grimaced. "That for me?"

He hoped not. The brownie looked as though it'd gone a few rounds with a vacuum cleaner.

"I made it for you," she said. "Well, Abby helped, but I did most of it."

She gazed up at him with such adoration, with such clear infatuation that panic slid up his spine.

He wasn't cut out to handle a prepubescent crush. He didn't have the patience needed to deal with a child's sensitive feelings. Had no clue how to handle someone looking at him as if he'd hung the damn moon.

He didn't want the burden of having someone feel so much for him.

"Thank you," he said solemnly as he took the brownie from her. It was still warm and bits of chocolate stuck to his palm. "I bet it's delicious. But you'd better get back to the kitchen. See if they need your help."

She grinned, and she was so cute with her sparkly shirt and glasses, how could he not smile back? "Bye," she said before doing some sort of cross between a skip and a jog out of the room.

As soon as she turned the corner, he stuffed the brownie behind the vase of flowers on the small table, grabbed his water and stepped onto the porch. The lights on either side of the door were on, dispelling any shadows and casting the house in a warm, welcoming light.

The clear day had given way to a clear evening. Stars dotted the sky; the moon's glow broke through the twilight. Matt breathed deeply of the crisp night air but it felt as if a weight lay on his chest. That's what being home did to him, made him feel as if he was suffocating.

As he shook out his arms and hopped from foot to foot in a prerun warm-up, Connie pulled her minivan to a stop in front of the house. He watched her climb out of the car and circle around to get something from the back. Seemed to him she was always moving. Always focusing on what needed to be done next. Slinging a small duffel bag over her shoulder, she shut the back of the van then walked toward him. Her strides, as usual, were long and quick, the energy around her palpable.

Stretching his right quad, he wondered what it would be like to have her focus all of that energy on him. To have her move around him. Over him. An unbidden image of her doing just that, of her lean, naked body rising over his, pierced his mind. He pushed it out again. But the memory lingered just outside his consciousness like some hazy dream. His pulse sped. Heat prickled his skin. His fingers went numb and his foot slipped from his grip, hitting the wooden porch floor with a thud.

He took a deep drink of water to soothe his dry throat.

Connie climbed the steps, a frown creasing her forehead as she slid her gaze over him. But she didn't comment on his attire—dark, loose windpants and a white, long-sleeved T-shirt.

"How's your mom?" he asked.

"Fine. Liz thinks it's just stress but wanted to keep her overnight for observation just to be on the safe side."

Liz Montgomery was not only Brady's ex-fiancée

and his current fiancée's older sister, but also a doctor in the E.R.

He glanced at his watch. Almost seven. "It took you this long for her to get looked at?"

"Yeah. It was crazy busy." She switched the duffel to her other arm and shivered. "We waited two hours before we even got put into a room."

Her face was pale, causing the dark smudges staining the delicate skin under her eyes to stand out in stark relief. She still wore the same sweatshirt she'd had on earlier, her jacket nowhere in sight. Her hair stood on end, as if she'd tried to finger comb away a case of hat-hair brought on by that scruffy ball cap she'd worn in the vineyard. A section stuck straight out above her ear. His fingers twitched with the need to smooth it down.

He curled them into his palms instead. "I'm glad it's not anything serious."

"Thanks." She glanced at the door as if debating an escape. But then she met his eyes. "How far did you all get with the pruning?"

"We got just over an acre of the Viognier finished."

"Good progress. I need to check my charts," she said, almost as if talking to herself, "see which grapes will be next in line."

"You keep a record of past years' bud breaks?"

Her mouth flattened. "Of course."

Smart. And exactly what he did, as well. By keeping a log of when each species of grape reached bud break, they could take into consideration the weather during past years and currently to help them decide the order in which to prune the vines.

If you want your working relationship with her to go smoothly, why don't you try listening to her, working with her instead of proving you know more.

"I'd like to go over those charts," he said slowly, Aidan's words echoing in his ears. "If you don't mind. Actually, it'd probably be best if we set up a meeting sometime this week so you can get me up to speed with everything going on with the vineyards. Spraying schedule. Equipment maintenance. Any soil testing you've done."

She bristled. "I already told you, I run things—"

"I know. You run the vineyard like Dad taught you. But he's not here. We are." He held her gaze, kept his voice light. Nonthreatening. "And you're no longer running things on your own. We're in this together."

It was only smart business to learn all he could about the Diamond Dust's vineyards, smarter yet to get that information from the woman who'd been a part of the company for so long, a woman who took great pride in her work. They'd go over her information, discuss ways to make the vineyards even better. And because he knew she was good at her job, he'd take her opinions under serious consideration.

But he'd still have the final say.

She closed the distance between them in a hip-swaying walk that made him feel as if he was being stalked. "Aidan tried to give me that same line about you and me being co-managers. I'm not buying it. But if going over how I do things proves to you that I'm a damn good vineyard manager, then I'll get my laptop from my office and we can have our little meeting tonight after dinner."

She moved to brush past him. He snagged her elbow. "I'm not staying for dinner."

"But…this whole family dinner is for you. Your mom is doing this for you."

His fingers tightened on Connie's arm before he released her. "She's hoping that now that she's suckered me into staying in Jewell that I'll slip right back into the family fold. Filling the space I left empty when I took off all those years ago."

The mold he had no desire to ever fit into again.

"Or maybe," Connie said, her tone biting, "she wants to have a nice dinner with all of her children present. Children she's rarely seen over the past ten years."

Guilt squeezed his chest. But he wasn't going to let her shame him. Not when he was in the right. He edged closer to Connie, forcing her to step back. "She blackmailed me. She coldly, ruthlessly went after what she wanted, not giving a damn how anyone else felt. And now she wants us all to be one big happy family. But she can't have it both ways. I don't work that way."

"Well, that's no surprise, seeing as how you're the king of holding grudges."

Only when they deserved to be held. "The only reason I gave in to Mom's threat was so the Diamond Dust can stay in the family. And because I did, my reputation, my whole career is on the line."

"Wow. Way to take one for the home team. I mean, poor you, being forced to work with your family and be part of an established, profitable company. The horror."

Frustration and fear boiled over. He gripped her elbows, lifting her to her toes. Her eyes widened, and she clenched his forearms. "Damn it. I could lose everything." He shook her once. "Everything."

His breathing ragged, his emotions tearing him up inside, he did the only thing he could think of.

He kissed her.

CHAPTER SEVEN

CONNIE'S GASP WAS SWALLOWED by Matt's warm, firm mouth.

Her fingers curled into his arms. Despite the cool evening temps, he was warm, his muscles bunching under her hands. His kiss was angry. A little mean. Desperate. And so very hot. It was as if he was burning up. For her.

Thoughts spun through her head. Told her to stop him. Now. Before whatever force he was exerting pulled her under.

But then he slipped his tongue between her lips, touched the tip of it to hers. And she sank under his spell with a low moan, her mind going blank.

He hauled her against him, one hand going to her hip, the other pulling her even closer at the small of her back as he took the kiss deeper. She slid her hands up his chest, the silky fabric of his shirt a cool contrast to his body heat. He was all solid, lean muscle and she was trapped between the cold, unforgiving wall and his hard body. Held hostage by the feel of his heart beating against her palm, the light rasp of his unshaven upper lip against hers.

Rising to her toes, she wound her arms around his

neck, her fingers delving into the thick, soft hair at his nape, the movement loosening the band holding it back. He lifted one hand, cupped the back of her head to hold her still as he changed the kiss. Slowed it down. Took it from hard and edgy to pure heat. Pure want.

Still kissing her, he slipped his hand under her sweat-shirt, softly scratched his nails up the narrow indentation at the base of her spine before smoothing around to her stomach. He trailed the rough pads of his fingers over the sensitive skin just above her belly button. Her muscles contracted.

Oh, dear Lord, the man could kiss. Like he had all day to explore her mouth, the taste and feel of her. The way his lips moved over hers, skilled, seductive, made it so easy to forget everything else. Someone like Matt did that, took his time, made a woman feel as if she was the only thing on his mind.

As if she was the only thing that mattered.

And for a few heated minutes, with Matt's hands on her, his hard body against hers, the taste of him on her tongue, she didn't worry about making anyone happy, or what anyone else wanted.

Which was exactly why that type of attention from a sexy man could get a girl in deep trouble. Especially one who had responsibilities. Who had people who counted on her to make the right decisions. To take care of them.

She tore her mouth from his, pushed against him until he lifted his head. He stared down at her, his eyes glittering in the pale porch light, his chest rising and falling heavily. The hair she'd tugged free of the band blew around his face, giving him a sexy, savage look.

Her mouth dried. She curled her hands into fists to stop from reaching for him again. Feeling cornered, panicked, she shoved at him once more. "Back up," she said, her tone too husky to be anywhere near intimidating. She cleared her throat. "Now."

He eased back, taking his time, but at least she was able to slip past him. Hugging her arms around herself, she walked toward the door, only to stumble over the bag she'd packed with the girls' pajamas. She righted herself, her cheeks heating.

"Should I apologize?" Matt asked, his voice harsh in the still night.

Turning, she studied him. His hands were on his narrow hips, his shirt clinging to the solid planes of his chest, pulled taut along his shoulders. "I guess that depends," she said finally, "on if you're sorry or not."

His grin was fast and razor sharp. "For kissing a beautiful woman? Can't say I've ever regretted that."

She rolled her eyes. "You can cut out the charming act. I'm many things, but beautiful isn't one of them."

"First of all," he said as he slowly closed the distance between them. "I don't have an act." It took all of her willpower not to step back. "Second, I'm the one looking at you." She froze, her breath caught in her chest as he lightly brushed the tip of his finger over the ends of her hair above her ear. "You're beautiful," he said softly.

Oh, God.

She inhaled shakily and stepped back as a car pulled

into the driveway, its headlights illuminating the porch. Connie picked up the bag at her feet. She couldn't let Matt's flattery and sexy innuendo get to her. He was too practiced in the art of saying whatever he needed to get his own way.

Then again, he hadn't said a word during their kiss and he'd held her mesmerized. Enough that she'd clung to him like some clichéd sex-starved divorcée while her daughters and his mother were getting dinner ready.

J.C. and Brady climbed out of J.C.'s tiny car. Slammed their doors shut.

Connie glanced at them then lifted her chin to Matt. "Well…" And having no idea what she could possibly say that would make her feel less idiotic, less desperate, she gave up and reached for the door.

"Running away?" he asked.

Damn right.

Her fingers tightened on the door handle. "Going to dinner. And letting you get on with your night."

"Oh, thank God we're not late," J.C. said, hurrying up the steps, her hair a wild mass of curls. "I fell asleep after work and Brady didn't wake me until fifteen minutes ago."

Brady followed more slowly. "You needed your rest." When she sent him a scorching look he just shrugged. "Relax. No one cares if we're a few minutes late for dinner."

"Your mother might care."

"Mom intimidates her," he told Matt as he reached the porch.

"Please," J.C. said derisively, "it's more like she scares the crap out of me."

Seeing her opportunity for a painless escape—one where she could keep what was left of her pride—Connie linked her arm with J.C.'s. "Come on. I'll protect you."

She opened the door, but before she could cross the threshold, Matt's voice stopped her.

"I'll come by your house tomorrow night then. To discuss the vineyard," he added when she sent him a startled glance over her shoulder. "Around seven work for you?"

What choice did she have? "Make it six," she said. "That way we'll be done before I have to get the girls ready for bed."

And as she went inside, she tried to convince herself that by tomorrow night she'd no longer be reeling from his kiss.

MATT STARED AT THE CLOSED door of his mother's house. His blood still thrummed heavily in his veins. He rubbed his thumb over the tips of his fingers but he could still feel the softness of her skin. For those few moments when Connie had been in his arms, it'd felt as if he'd been able to breathe. And he wanted, more than anything, to get that feeling back again.

"Everything okay with Connie?" Brady asked.

Matt turned to see his brother scrutinizing him as if he could look into his head and read his mind.

He shifted his weight from foot to foot, realized

he was fidgeting and forced himself to stand still. "Why?"

"She seemed upset."

"Of course she's upset," he growled. "She just spent half the day with her mom in the E.R."

"Is Margaret okay?"

"Far as I know. They admitted her for observation."

Brady tucked his fingers into his back pockets. Though he only had on a short-sleeved T-shirt and jeans, he showed no signs the cold bothered him. "That why you were touching Connie's hair?"

Matt's own hair blew in his face, reminding him half of it had come loose. Yanking the band out—and with it, several strands of hair—he glared at Brady. "What?"

"I saw you when we pulled in."

He tipped his head to the side until his neck popped. "So I kissed her. You have a problem with that?"

Brady's eyebrows rose fractionally. "You kissed her?"

Matt nodded.

"You kissed Connie Henkel," Brady repeated. "As in *kissed her* kissed her?"

"Want me to draw you a goddamn diagram?"

"She's not your usual type."

Matt took a menacing step forward. Brady just gave him a bland look.

"I don't have a type," Matt said, "when it comes to women." Especially sexy women with long legs and deep blue eyes and a quick and mobile mouth. "I'm all about equal opportunity."

The door opened. Both men glanced over as J.C. stuck her head out. "Are you coming?" she asked her fiancé. "We're almost ready to eat."

"In a minute," Brady said, then waited for her to shut the door again. "There's nothing easy about Connie. And you're all about easy."

And didn't that sum up his entire family's view of him? The only Sheppard to take the easy way out.

"Not always," he rasped. "I'm here, aren't I? There's nothing easy about this situation."

Brady didn't seem to hear the edge to Matt's voice or, more likely, chose to ignore it. "You didn't want to figure out how to get along with Dad so you went to a college on the other side of the country."

"I went to UC Davis because its viticulture and enology program is one of the best in the country."

The fact it was in California was just a side benefit. One that he was thankful for after that last fight with his father.

"You never search for jobs," his brother continued. "You wait until one falls into your lap. If they don't, you shrug and find something else to do until the next one comes along. Same with women."

He fisted his hands, his arms trembling as anger surged. Unlike what his family thought, he did not sit back and wait for jobs to fall from the freaking sky. It'd taken him years to build his reputation. Years of hard dedicated work to gain the notice of the most prestigious wineries. And now that he had? He drummed his fingers on his thigh. He had to throw it all away to save his family's collective asses.

"Which is why you and Connie comes as a surprise," Brady continued. "I wouldn't have guessed that one."

Matt about choked on his own spit. "There's no me and Connie. There's no me and any woman. At least, not any one woman."

"You're a regular Casanova. But since you don't have a thing for Connie—"

"I don't."

He didn't have *things* for women. If he was attracted to a woman and that feeling was mutual, he acted on it. Period. And when that attraction faded, as it always did, they both went their separate ways. There were too many rules to relationships. Too many compromises he wasn't willing to make.

Brady shifted his weight to his good leg. "You're just killing time, then?"

"It was a kiss. Not a marriage proposal. Or any kind of proposal."

Brady studied Matt. "Want my advice?"

"Not particularly."

"Stay away from her."

Faking an ease he didn't feel, Matt stretched his arms overhead. "Hard to do if I'm stuck here. Unless you plan on firing her."

"I don't mean avoid her, I mean *stay away* from her."

Matt rolled his eyes. "Great clarification. You sure have a way with words there, Hemingway."

Brady didn't blink. Sometimes Matt thought his brother really was made of stone. "Don't kiss her again. Don't flirt with her. Or watch her when you think no one else is looking."

"I don't—"

"And don't sleep with her."

A flash of heat burned through him. An image of Connie, all long limbs and soft skin filled his mind.

He shook his head. "I hadn't planned on sleeping with her." Then again, he hadn't planned on kissing her, either.

Aw, hell.

"Good," Brady said with a slight nod. "And while I can appreciate you enjoying nothing more than pissing off Aidan, I don't think it's a good idea in this case."

"I should've known he'd have a No Fraternization Between Employees policy."

"He doesn't." Brady frowned thoughtfully. "Not that I know of anyway. He's just…protective of Connie."

At the idea of Aidan protecting Connie, bitterness filled Matt's mouth. He hadn't noticed Aidan looking at her in any particular way, but then again, he wasn't around much. Plus his eldest brother always had been excellent at hiding his true feelings.

His fingers curled and he tucked them behind his back. Out of Brady's eagle-eyed sight. "You saying Aidan and Connie…?"

"No." *Idiot.* His brother didn't say it but he sure as hell implied it. "Not every relationship between a man and a woman is sexual."

Matt's lips curved. "Good one. Glad to see you found a sense of humor at long last."

"They're friends," he said, speaking slowly as if Matt was a banana short of a fruit salad. "They've worked here, closely, for years. Plus, she and Mom are tight. Think of the problems it'll cause for you, for everyone, if you and Connie were to get involved."

Matt tried to look innocent. "Is that supposed to be a euphemism for something?"

Brady sighed. "Look, no matter how on board she might be with a no-strings-attached fling, when you leave, people will get pissed. Or worse. Hurt."

"I don't get to leave," Matt said, unable to hide his resentment. "Remember? I have to stick around for the unforeseeable future."

"Once the year's up, you'll be gone. You know it. I know it. Aidan knows it. Even Mom knows it…though she probably won't admit it to herself."

"So what you're saying is you're not counting on me to go through with the partnership?" He kept his voice deceptively lazy though the words seemed to burn his throat.

"You'll go through with it," Brady said, heading for the door. "For the year. And then you'll go your own way again."

And his brother went inside.

What was so bad about going one's own way? About living life for himself instead of jumping through hoops for other people. If that made him a selfish bastard, then so be it. Damn it, he was smart. Independent. And he'd made something of himself on his own.

You'll come back, his dad had said that night when Matt had thought he was finally free of the Diamond Dust forever. *And when you do, I'll be waiting.*

Yeah. Waiting to rub Matt's failure in his face. Except he hadn't failed.

And his father hadn't lived long enough to see he'd been wrong about his youngest son.

"IF WE HIRE A HALF DOZEN teenagers," Matt said the next night as he sat across from Connie at her small kitchen table, "we can cut our pruning time down by a third."

"And have a bunch of kids trampling around, hacking my vineyards to bits?" She shook her head. "No way." She leaned forward, pointed at the calendar she'd made of the pruning schedule. "If we stay on track, we'll be finished in three weeks. If we want to speed things up, we can ask Aidan and your mom to pitch in. At least that way we know it's being done correctly."

Pruning, like making wine, was an art and a science. It took knowledge and practice to know how much growth to leave. A sufficient number of buds needed to be on the plant to have a decent crop load, but not so many that the plant couldn't sustain them or the buds wouldn't ripen.

"How about we compromise," he suggested, leaning back in his chair and linking his hands on top of his head. "We hire a kid to work part-time after school and on weekends, one who can drive the tractor. He can handle all the grunt work like mowing and spreading compost." He shrugged, the movement causing his light blue shirt to stretch across his chest. "That'll free up one of the full-time crew so they concentrate on the vines."

Damn it, it wasn't a bad idea. They'd been going over everything from her spraying schedule to what material she was using in her compost to those soil analyses she'd gotten back earlier in the week.

From what she'd learned tonight, Aidan had been right about Matt. He was good at what he did.

And it would've been so much easier if he wasn't. Or if his wine philosophy ran counter to the Diamond Dust's, which was to make wines with character by tending the vineyards by hand to express the quality of the terroir and using sustainable farming techniques. Instead, Matt seemed to care as much as anyone in his family for those tenets on which the Diamond Dust had been founded.

So he was capable, knowledgeable and, most important, had the last name Sheppard. He would be a more than efficient and successful vineyard manager for the business. And where would that leave her?

"We'll have to discuss it with Aidan first," she said, avoiding Matt's eyes by gathering the calendar pages. "If he goes for it, I can put an ad in the paper starting next week."

He lowered his arms. "Sounds good."

"Mom," Abby called from the doorway, "Payton keeps watching TV instead of doing her homework."

"Nu-uh," Payton insisted as she joined her sister.

"You know you're not to have the television on while you're doing homework," Connie said.

Payton bided her time by adjusting her glasses. "I must've accidentally pushed the On button when I moved the remote."

"Amazing," Connie said dryly while Matt coughed, no doubt to cover a laugh. "Don't tell me, the channel just happened to switch to *SpongeBob Squarepants*."

"Weird, huh?" Payton asked, all wide-eyed innocence.

God help her, Connie thought, when Payton hit her teens.

"Bring your homework in here," she told her girls as she closed her laptop. "We were just finishing up, anyway." She glanced at Matt. "Unless there's something else you want to go over?"

He sat up. "I think that's good for tonight. I appreciate you letting me interrupt your evening like this."

She just shrugged. As if she had a choice after the way he'd cornered her last night in front of J.C. and Brady. She'd noticed the speculation in Brady's eyes and hadn't wanted to do anything to add to his suspicions. So at six on the dot, she'd opened her front door to Matt.

They'd spent almost two hours discussing the winery. Two hours of sitting across from him pretending she wasn't ready to jump out of her skin every time she caught him watching her with his intense gaze.

Pretending she hadn't spent a restless night reliving their kiss.

The girls came into the kitchen carrying their books and pencils. Payton gazed adoringly at Matt as she took the seat next to him. Seemed his charms worked well on the under-ten set. Not that Connie could blame her daughter. With his hair waving around his face, his cheeks covered in gold stubble, he looked all sorts of sexy and dangerous and more appealing than any man had a right to.

She picked up her laptop to make room for Abby's math workbook while Matt stood and crossed to the sink to rinse out his coffee cup.

"Mommy," Payton asked as she meticulously laid out her English worksheet, a blank sheet of paper and a pencil, "can I have a bowl of Lucky Charms?"

"Sure." She set the laptop on the antique washstand she'd found at a flea market a month before her divorce. "Abby, you want some, too?"

Abby sent a furtive glance Matt's way then shook her head. Payton had skipped across the room and taken the box of cereal out from the bottom cupboard.

"Could you help me get a bowl?" Payton asked Matt. "I can't reach." She sent him a beseeching look, complete with batted eyelashes, and pointed to the upper cabinet where the cereal bowls sat stacked on the second shelf.

The same upper cabinet she got a bowl from every day.

As soon as Matt left, Connie and her daughters were

having a very serious discussion about not pretending to be helpless so a man would save them. About how important it was to be strong and independent and not rely on anyone else to take care of them.

Like she'd relied on their father to take care of her.

"Why don't you use the stool?" Abby asked, carefully writing the answer to one of her equations. "Like always."

Poor Payton's cheeks turned so red, she looked like her face had caught fire. Before she could respond to her sister, though, Matt opened the cupboard and took down a bowl.

Then he smiled at her. "Here you go, short stuff." And he winked at her.

Clutching the bowl to her chest as if he'd just given her the most precious of gifts, Payton let out a dreamy sigh. "Thank you."

Good God, Connie was so not ready for this. She hadn't planned on having to deal with her daughter's first case of puppy love for a few more years. She wanted those years. Needed them to somehow figure out how to protect her baby from getting her heart broken.

"Good luck with that homework," Matt said as he followed Connie into the living room.

She went to the small closet where she'd hung up his jacket when he'd arrived. The leather was as soft as butter and his spicy scent clung to it. It was all she could do not to press her face to the collar and sniff it.

"Thanks for being a good sport with Payton," she

said as she handed him his coat. "A girl's first crush is a major event in her life."

"You remember your first crush?"

"Brian Karnes," she said without hesitation. "He was sixteen and our paperboy. I was twelve and convinced we belonged together."

Putting his jacket on, he smiled. "You didn't have your first crush until you were twelve? Late bloomer?"

"Actually, I think Payton's just advanced for her age. But there's one thing we have in common—we both fell for a pretty face."

"You have no idea how happy that makes me," he murmured as he edged closer to her, his husky tone making her knees weak. "You thinking I'm pretty."

Her heart thudded against her chest. All day while they'd pruned the vines with the rest of the crew, and even tonight in the relative privacy of her kitchen, he'd been professional. Friendly. There had been no flirting, no innuendos, nothing to indicate he'd had so much as a second thought about their kiss.

But from the heat in his eyes, he was thinking about it now, and wouldn't mind a repeat performance.

She swallowed. "Well, unfortunately, as with most crushes, Brian and I weren't meant to be. Too bad it took me eight months of waking up at 5:00 a.m. just so I could watch Brian deliver the paper before I realized we'd never work out. He was a skinny teenager with a Huffy bike and a mullet hairdo. And I...I was looking for my Prince Charming, someone to sweep in and rescue me…." And she was babbling. She pressed her hands against her cheeks in an effort to cool them.

"I'm no Prince Charming," he said so seriously, so adamantly, some of her nervousness dissipated.

"I don't think you have to worry about that. Payton's not looking for her prince, just a part-time father figure."

Matt blanched and took a step back, fear and horror on his face. As if she'd just yelled *catch* and thrown a newborn his way.

"You…your ex…Phil—"

"Paul," she corrected.

"Right. He's not around the girls much?"

She smoothed her hair behind her ear. "Paul does the best he can but since he moved to Tennessee, he only gets to see the girls one weekend a month plus two weeks in the summer."

Matt scowled. "He lives that far from his own kids?"

"He got a VP position at a factory in Knoxville. With the promotion and the pay increase, it was too good of an opportunity to pass up."

At least, that's what Paul had told her when he'd first received the offer five years into their marriage. And then he'd explained that he was going to Knoxville alone. They'd drifted apart, he'd said. So why bother pretending there was anything left in their marriage to save? It'd be easier, quicker and less painful if they just moved on with their lives. Separately. He'd start a new life in Knoxville and she and the girls could stay in Jewell.

And though it'd hurt her pride to admit it, he'd been right. Any love she'd told herself she'd felt for him had long since withered away. She'd expected too much from him.

"Both girls have a good relationship with Paul," she continued. "I just think Payton's going through a stage where she's looking for someone more accessible."

But if she was looking at Matt to fill that void in her life, she was making a huge mistake. Sure, he was here now, had committed to staying in Jewell for at least a year, but Connie didn't believe for one minute he'd stick around. After all, three hundred and sixty-five days was practically forever to a man like Matt.

And she didn't doubt that on day three hundred and sixty-six, he would be long gone.

CHAPTER EIGHT

Matt wondered what had put that sadness in Connie's eyes. If it was there for her daughter—or herself.

But he didn't ask. It was easier, safer, to keep things on a casual level. He liked his connections with people loose. That way he could free himself quickly and effortlessly when the time came to leave.

"I'm flattered to be considered crush material," he said mildly, as if the idea of Payton pinning her hopes and dreams on him didn't have him breaking out in a cold sweat. "And to be in the same league as mullet-head Brian Karnes."

The way Connie studied him, her brows lowered, her eyes serious, made him feel as if she could somehow read his thoughts. See inside his soul to who he really was.

And found him sorely lacking.

"Yes, well, not many guys could pull off the mullet—especially with hair as curly as Brian's—but he managed." She gave him an uncertain smile. "But don't worry too much about Payton's infatuation with you. I'm sure it won't last long."

"You females and your fickle affections," he said dryly as the phone rang.

Now her smile widened, reaching her eyes. "During childhood we're fickle," she admitted as the phone's second ring was abruptly cut off. "As adults we prefer to think of it as being more discriminating."

"Mom!" Payton called from the kitchen. "Phone. It's Grandma."

And just like that, her smile slid away. Her shoulders tensed. "Sorry," she said, crossing to the cordless phone on the end table. "I need to take this."

"No problem. I'll see you in the morning."

Having already picked up the phone, she just nodded. "Hi, Mom," she said. "Everything okay?"

"Mommy," Abby said as she came into the living room, her feet bare, a sheet of paper in her hands, "I'm all done with my math and need you to help me practice my spelling."

Connie held up a *wait-a-minute* finger. "Mom," he heard her say as he walked away. "Mom. You need to slow down. I'm having a hard time understanding you."

"Mom-my," Abby whined, "you said I couldn't watch *iCarly* until my homework's done and it'll be on soon."

Matt opened the door, stared out into the dark night. The company truck he'd driven was parked across the street, the Diamond Dust logo illuminated by a streetlight.

"You're just going to have to wait until I'm off the phone," Connie said in a loud whisper—presumably to Abby.

"But you said—"

"Abigail, you will sit down and be quiet until I'm off the phone," Connie said evenly, but underneath he heard a note of resignation, of exhaustion that left him unable to move.

Fresh air washed over him, beckoned him to just walk away. At that very moment, millions of these little domestic dramas were being played out in homes all over the world. This wasn't anything unique or momentous. Connie could handle this on her own. Seemed to him, she handled everything on her own. Raising her daughters. Caring for her mother.

Who took care of her?

He squeezed the door handle before forcing his fingers to let go. Then he shut the door. "I'll do it." At Connie's questioning frown he explained, "I'll help Abby with her spelling. Get her out of your hair so you can finish your conversation."

Frowning, Connie covered the mouthpiece. "That's really nice of you to offer," she said, "but it's not necessary." She paused, took her hand away. "No, Mom. Not you. Could you hold on for one second?" This time she pressed the phone against her chest. "I usually read the words to her and she writes them—"

"It'll be fine." You'd think he'd offered to help the kid study for med school. She was in, what…first grade? How hard could it be? "Any big words I can't sound out myself, I'm sure the girls can help me with."

Connie still looked unsure, which pissed him off to no end. It wasn't as if he was riding to her rescue or anything. He was just helping her and the kid out. Because he'd interrupted their usual evening routine by insisting Connie go over her management style with him, show him how she ran the vineyards.

Prove to him that she was good enough to work with him.

Maybe Aidan was right. Maybe he really was an arrogant bastard.

Finally Connie nodded. "Okay. Thanks."

"Come on, short stuff," Matt said to Abby as he headed back to the kitchen.

She slid off the couch and hurried after him. "That's what you call Payton."

"It is?" he asked, stopping just outside the kitchen.

She nodded with an expectant expression, as if she was looking for something from him. The idea of which made him twitchy. As if he had an itch he couldn't reach.

"You could call me something else," Abby whispered. "If you wanted."

He glanced down at her. Sticking her thumb in her mouth, she stared at him through her lashes. And he remembered being around her age, following his father around the vineyard. Happy to be anywhere, to be doing anything, as long as he was with his dad. Wanting nothing more than some individual attention away from his brothers.

"If your sister is Short Stuff, then I guess that would make you Shorter Stuff, huh?" She grinned shyly, still not taking her thumb from her mouth. "No? How about Munchkin, then?"

She grinned hugely. "Okay."

He felt as if he'd just won some sort of prize. He held out his hand. "Now, let's see that list."

At the table, Payton was drinking from her cereal bowl. She lowered it, leaving behind a milk mustache. "You're still here."

"He's helping me with my spelling," Abby said with a noticeable trace of pride.

"I have spelling homework." Payton wiped the back of her hand over her lip then dug into a backpack on the table. "Can you help me, too?"

"Sure." Maybe this whole domestic shtick wasn't so bad. In small doses. He sat next to Abby. "Ready?"

She nodded, her expression serious, a pencil gripped tightly in her hand. Damn, but she was a cute little thing. And the way she frowned reminded him of her mother.

"First word is *after*."

She bent her head, her ponytail sliding forward to trail along the tabletop, and slowly wrote the word.

"Found it," Payton cried as she jumped down from her seat and came around the table. She set her homework in front of him then leaped back, lifted her arms above her head and twirled around twice, stumbling at the end but managing to avoid falling on her rear.

"Whoa. Those are quite the moves you've got there," he said.

"I'm in dance class." She pushed her glasses back up her nose. "Do you like ballet?"

Before he could respond, Abby spoke in a small voice. "I'm ready."

"Right. Next word—" He quickly found his place on the spelling list. *"Camper."*

"Do you?" Payton asked.

He shook his head. Did he what? Oh, right. Ballet. "I don't think I'd look so good in tights," he deadpanned. "Or one of those tutu things."

Payton giggled, the sound tugging at his heart. "Not do you like to dance ballet. Do you like to watch it?"

And for some reason the hope in her eyes made him nervous. As if his answer to this question was really important to her. And damned if he needed that kind of pressure.

He didn't want this little girl to pin her hopes on him. Not when he was used to only worrying about his own dreams.

"It's not my favorite," he said slowly, "but it's okay."

"If you wanted, you could come to my dance re-cital."

Wincing at the note of excitement in her voice, he ducked his head and hoped she hadn't noticed. "When is it?"

"I'm not sure of the date, but it'll be in May."

Three months from now. Unless it was for a job, he never made plans further than a few days. Except now he knew exactly where he'd be in three…six… even nine months. Exactly what he'd be doing. Living in

Jewell. Working at the Diamond Dust. Trying to fulfill the wishes of a dead man.

Bitterness burned in his throat. He knew what life here was like and he didn't want it. Didn't want anything to do with the whole small-town domestic scene of dealing with parents and kids' recitals and homework. Of having people count on him. Of facing their disappointment when he failed to live up to their expectations.

"You're getting my paper all wrinkly," Abby said, touching his arm with her small, soft hand.

He shook his head then realized he was crumpling her spelling list in his tight fists. "Sorry," he muttered, smoothing the corners with unsteady fingers. "Next word is *shower.*"

"I'll send you an invitation to the recital," Payton was saying, oblivious to his silent freak-out. "We get to invite two extra people other than our moms and dads so that means you and Diane can come."

Panic had him practically jumping out of his chair. "You know what?" he asked, already backing up toward the door. "I...just remembered there's something I have to do."

Payton followed. "What?"

"I have to feed my dog," he blurted. Terror seized him at the thought of having either of these sweet little girls depending on him for anything more than a stupid nickname or lame joke. "Well, technically it's my brother's dog so I should just...go."

Then he bailed.

"I JUST DON'T UNDERSTAND," Margaret was saying as Connie paced in front of the sofa, "why Dr. Tweet wants to send some horrible stranger over here. I know what he's doing," she continued breathlessly. "He wants to put me in some home so he can take all my money. My freedom. You won't let that happen, will you, Constance? You wouldn't let them force me out of my own home."

As their conversation had progressed, Margaret's voice had risen and fallen only to rise again. She was now speaking quickly, her breathing ragged after ten minutes of nonstop complaining and whining about her psychiatrist ordering a visiting nurse to check on her at home.

"Mom, I need you to calm down and listen to me, okay?" She struggled to keep her tone soothing. As if she wasn't two seconds from yanking her hair out by the fistful. "No one is after your money." Of which there wasn't much. Margaret received state assistance along with whatever Connie could spare. "Dr. Tweet is sending a nurse over as a precaution. Remember? He explained to both of us that he just wants to make sure you're safe in the house alone and taking your medicines correctly."

Connie was grateful for the doctor's help with her mother. Especially since Margaret's condition had worsened over the past two years.

"Will you be here when she comes?" Margaret asked, sounding like a scared child.

Still pacing, Connie explained. "I have to work, remember? But I'll be over in the morning like always and I'll be sure to stop by after work, as well."

When she reached the end table, she jumped when Matt came out of the kitchen and bolted for the door without sparing her a glance.

"I have to go," she said quickly to her mom. "I'll see you in the morning." Hating to cut Margaret off but knowing she'd never get her mother off the phone otherwise, she didn't wait for a response, just hung up.

By the time she hurried across the room to the door, Matt was racing down her porch steps. "What happened?" she called, forcing him to stop on the sidewalk. "Don't tell me those second grade spelling words were too much for you?"

He didn't move, just stood there with his back to her, his hands fisted at his sides. She stepped onto the porch, shivered violently as the cold seeped through her thin socks and bit into her skin. Turning to pull the door shut behind her, she noticed her girls standing in the living room wide-eyed.

"Back to that homework," she told them evenly, as if it was every day a gorgeous man hung out at their house and offered to read spelling words, then ran off as if the girls had lit his head on fire.

Since he didn't seem in any hurry to turn around—or come closer to her—Connie crossed her arms against the chill and went to him. Walking carefully on her toes down the rough, uneven sidewalk, she skirted around him.

"You okay?" she asked.

He didn't move. Just stared over her head as if gauging if he could get past her and to his truck. The streetlight cast his features in stark relief, made his face seem more angular. His jaw sharper, his eyes colder.

"I don't want this," he said quietly, still not looking at her. "None of it."

"Want to give me a clue what *this* is?"

He finally met her eyes but she couldn't read what was in his. "I don't want this—" He gestured at her house then pointed back and forth between them. "The whole small-town life. Kids and homework and the same routine day after day."

"Funny, but I don't remember proposing," she said, her fury so great her voice shook. But she welcomed that anger, the flash of heat that scorched through her bloodstream. "You know, just when I start to think maybe you're not some smug, arrogant prick, you prove me wrong."

Before she could walk away, he snatched her by the elbow. "Now, just a goddamn minute—"

"You think you can stand here outside of my home and look down on me and my children? On how we live our lives?" She hated that her voice was thick with unshed tears.

His eyes widened and his fingers tightened on her arm. "Wait… No. That's not what I…" He tipped his head back, inhaled deeply. When he lowered it again, his voice was calmer, though his hold on her was still firm. "That's not what I meant."

She yanked free, stumbling with the force of her

movement, but when he reached out to steady her, she slapped his hand. "It's exactly what you meant. What I don't understand is where you get off judging the way I choose to live my life when, from where I'm standing, your own is the one that needs work."

A muscle in his jaw jerked. "My life was fine…perfect…until my mother came up with her ultimatum." He stalked toward her. Her pulse kicked up but she held her ground. Still, he grew closer until she had to tip her head back to maintain eye contact. "Do you have any idea what I've had to give up? I had to renege on the most lucrative contract of my career. All my plans, all my dreams of the future, of one day having a winery of my own—of my own, not one started by my father—are all gone now."

His voice was so raw, so angry and…lost. Some of her anger seeped away. Because he was right. He did have to give up a lot in order to keep the Diamond Dust in the family. Before now, she hadn't really considered exactly how much. She'd been so focused on how unfair this situation was to her, she hadn't cared that maybe, just maybe, it might be unfair to Matt, too.

But, as she often told her girls when they didn't get their own way, life was unfair. She knew that better than anyone, and yet, she still did her best each day to make the most of what she did have.

"Does what your mother did to you, to all of you, suck?" she asked. "You bet. But she loves you. I can't help but believe she honestly thinks she's doing what's best. I'd…" She brushed her hair off her forehead, her fingers trembling. "God, I'd give anything to have what you have."

He stared down at her, his windblown hair and slitted eyes making him look sexier. More dangerous. "If it was up to me, you could have it."

Deflated, she let her shoulders sag. Yeah, if it was up to either of them, they'd both have what they wanted. She'd have the Diamond Dust. And he'd have his freedom.

She bit the inside of her cheek. Hard. His worst nightmare would be a dream come true for her. If she had been born a Sheppard.

"What are you looking for, Matt? Do you want me to feel sorry for you?" she asked wearily. "Because that's just not going to happen."

He bristled, edging closer, forcing her to lean back to avoid contact with his body. "I don't need anyone's pity, sugar."

"No? Because you sure seem to want it. You wear your resentment like a crown—big enough, shiny enough for the world to see. You've been given a chance to be a part of something you can call your own. You want to build a reputation? Build it here. Living in Jewell, working at the Diamond Dust isn't exactly the end of the world. And who knows?" she asked softly. "Maybe you'll gain more than you could ever imagine."

Then she walked away from the man who was being given everything she'd ever wanted and shut the door with a soft click.

WHAT DID SHE THINK? Matt wondered furiously as he pulled away from Connie's house. That he should be some freaking optimist who saw his current wineglass as half-full?

His pulse pounded in his ears but it couldn't cover the sound of Connie's voice.

I'd give anything to have what you have.

His fingers tightened on the wheel. She only said that because she'd had such a shitty childhood. Her dad had taken off when she was young, leaving her alone with a mentally ill mother. Growing up, she'd had no one to turn to, no other family.

Except his.

He'd been around eleven when Connie had first started working at the Diamond Dust, a sixteen-year-old with a bad attitude, a perpetual sneer and a penchant for running with the wrong crowd. But all that changed when his dad took her under his wing. She'd had his time, attention and, unlike Matt, she'd had his love.

To her, Tom Sheppard had been some sort of hero.

Matt turned onto the lane that would take him back to the Diamond Dust. But Connie had never had to sit through one of his father's lectures. Never had to hear what a disappointment she was to him.

Instead of parking the truck in the garage bay at the winery, Matt drove past it, not stopping until he got to his mother's house. Shutting off the ignition, he rested his forearms on the steering wheel and leaned forward. The tall, stately windows and porch were ablaze with warm, welcoming light.

As a kid, he used to sit on that porch and think about all the previous generations of Sheppards who'd lived there before him. How his father, grandfather and great-grandfather had once been his age. Had run through the same fields, raced up the same set of stairs, stared at the stars through the same bedroom window. It was just a house. Just wood and glass and cement. It shouldn't mean more than that.

So how did it have the power to make him feel like that little kid again? To make him relive countless memories, both good and bad, when all he wanted was to focus on the future.

He opened the door and had one foot on the ground when his cell phone rang. Seeing the out-of-country number he slid back onto the seat and shut the door again. "Hello?"

"It's Joan," she said in her rapid-fire way. "Any chance you've come to your senses?"

"I'm afraid not."

"Well, then, you give me no choice. I had my attorney draw up a breach of contract notice yesterday. I'll be sending it on to you."

He should've known Joan wouldn't waste any time trying to get even for his desertion. The worst part? He couldn't blame her. "I don't suppose there's any way we could settle this without getting the courts involved?"

Without dragging his name and his reputation through the mud.

"That's not how I work. When someone goes back

on their word to me," she said, her lyrical accent and tough words at odds, "they pay for it."

And she hung up.

Fantastic.

He slowly, carefully shut off his phone. Set it on the bench seat beside him before pushing his hair back from his face with both hands. He tried to concentrate on breathing through his frustration. His feelings of helplessness.

When that didn't work, he hit the dash with the heel of his hand. Again. And again. By the time he was done, his heart was racing, sweat lined his upper lip and a three-inch crack had formed in the hard plastic above the radio.

CHAPTER NINE

SOME POP TUNE ABOUT LOOSENING up buttons played from the CD player, the sound competing with the hoots and hollers of the dozen or so stag party attendees. Matt figured they were lucky to have that many show, given that Brady hadn't lived in Jewell for twelve years. And the guy was hardly Mr. Personality, even now that he was sober and working through his issues with PTSD.

To be honest, Matt was surprised anyone showed up.

The ones who were there were enjoying the long-legged blonde as she shook and shimmied her way around the makeshift dance floor. Seeing as how she wore a two-piece leather outfit, thigh-high fishnet stockings and red ankle boots with ice pick heels, there wasn't much not to enjoy.

"He hasn't moved in five minutes," Matt said, nodding at Brady, who sat scowling in the middle of the room, his shoulders stiff, his eyes straight ahead as the blonde bent over in front of him and wiggled her ass. "Is it possible to be catatonic and still have your eyes open?"

"He's not slipping into a coma." Aidan, dressed in his version of stag-party casual—pressed khakis and a button-down shirt, sans tie and with the sleeves rolled up—leaned back against the bar. "He's mad. He told you no strippers."

Matt sipped from the bottle of water he'd switched to an hour ago after his second beer. "She's not a stripper. She's an exotic dancer."

"She took her clothes off."

True. She had taken off the military-inspired costume she'd worn—a nice tribute, Matt thought, to Brady's time in the service. "Ah, but she left bits and pieces on. And therein lies the difference."

Aidan shot him one of his patented *you are such an ass* looks then went back to watching the show. They stayed that way for a few more bars of the song until Aidan said, "About this breach of contract matter—"

"How'd you—" Matt broke off and glared at the guest of honor. Son of a bitch. He'd confided in Brady because he thought he could trust him. "Brady's got a big mouth."

"Yes. We all know what a chatterbox he is," Aidan said dryly. "He thought we should know."

"We?"

"Mom and I." He frowned as their very married cousin David drunkenly slipped money into the waistband of the dancer's short-shorts. "The Diamond Dust will foot your legal fees and pay any restitution you may owe."

He squeezed the bottle, denting the plastic. "No, thanks."

Aidan didn't spare him a glance. "I wasn't asking

your permission. I was telling you how it's going to be. Deal with it." And then he walked away.

He'd deal with it all right, Matt thought as he drank his water. And though the Diamond Dust—and his mother—were directly responsible for him being sued, he'd handle it the way he handled everything else. On his own.

Pushing away his irritation, he leaned back against the bar and took in the party. They'd done the whole wedding rehearsal thing earlier in the evening, complete with dinner afterward. And while Brady hadn't been thrilled with the idea of a stag, Matt and Aidan had insisted. They'd kept it simple. Just rented out the back room of The Empire bar, ordered some items from the menu for them to snack on and paid for an open bar for the guests. Nothing wild. Nothing illegal or crazy and therefore nothing Brady could complain about.

And if he did complain about having a half-dressed woman dancing around him, he was even worse off than Matt had feared.

When the dancer undulated her hips in front of him, Brady stood and said something into her ear. She grinned hugely, nodded and began spreading her attention to the other men in the room, freeing Brady to cross to the bar.

"What was that all about?" Matt asked when Brady reached him.

"I told her she was doing such a great job, you were going to double any tips she made." He got the bartender's attention and ordered a soda. "Hope you brought cash to pay for this shindig."

He hadn't, but he could always hit the ATM. "It's worth it. Especially your expression when she walked in and told you Uncle Sam wanted you. I even recorded it—" he patted his phone in his pocket "—just in case J.C. wants to see how you enjoyed your party."

Brady responded with his middle finger.

Matt shrugged. "Next time have Aidan plan your stag. I was just trying to inject a little excitement into your last night as a free man."

"I've had a lifetime of excitement," he said, picking up the glass the bartender set on the counter. "I'm ready for some normalcy."

Normal. The whole house and picket fence and wife and kids thing. Routines. Schedules. Like what Connie had with her girls.

You think you can stand here outside of my home and look down on me and my children? On how we live our lives?

He straightened. Shoved her voice out of his head.

In Matt's mind, once you'd wrung all you could out of life, then, and only then, was the time to settle down. *Settle* being the operative word.

Then again, Brady had lived through more than his fair share of excitement fighting terrorists in Afghanistan. And he'd always been the kind of guy who'd been looking for a commitment, hence his years-long engagement to J.C.'s sister before Liz finally broke it off. Matt couldn't understand the urge himself, but if that's what the guy wanted...

He lifted his water. "Here's to normalcy, then."

Brady hesitated a moment then tapped his glass to Matt's bottle. "Thanks. And thanks for the party."

"Just doing my duty as head usher."

Aidan had been chosen as the best man. Not that it bothered Matt. Being best man came with a host of responsibilities and headaches he'd rather do without. No, he was much happier in his small role—his biggest stress tomorrow would be walking guests down the aisle without tripping anyone.

J.C.'s dad walked up to them. "Brady," Don Montgomery said, his round face flushed, either from the heat in the room or from the dancer shaking her generous breasts in his direction. "I'm heading out."

Brady straightened, offered his hand to his future father-in-law. "Thank you for coming, Dr. Montgomery."

"Of course. Wouldn't have missed it." Don shook Brady's hand, his tone making it clear that if he could have missed it, he would have. "I'll see you at the church tomorrow."

Even to Matt's ears that sounded like a question and a threat rolled into one.

"Yes, sir," Brady said. "Good night, sir."

Don nodded at Matt then walked away.

"That there is a man who does not like you," Matt noted.

"I showed up drunk at one daughter's wedding. Got

his other daughter pregnant." He took a drink. "I'm lucky he doesn't gut me like a fish."

"Brother, I'm glad I'm not you." For more reasons than Matt could ever list. "You sure you want to go through with this?"

Brady slid a narrow glance his brother's way. "Tell me you're not asking if I want to change my mind about my wedding. The wedding that's to take place in—" he checked his watch "—eighteen hours."

"Hey, you and J.C. could still be together. Still raise the baby together. But you wouldn't have to be in a situation where you have to spend your holidays sitting at the table with your father-in-law, who can't stand you, the woman you were once engaged to and her husband. You remember, the guy who broke you up in the first place?" He shook his head in pity. "I'm just saying it's a lot to put up with."

But Brady didn't seem worried about his new family dynamic. Actually, he no longer seemed to be listening to what Matt considered some excellent points. Instead, he was looking behind Matt toward the door that led to The Empire's main barroom with an intensity Matt had never seen before.

"J.C.'s worth it," he said.

Matt followed his gaze and saw a small group of women of various ages standing in the doorway, J.C. in the middle. She had on the same bright blue dress she'd worn to the wedding rehearsal, the shiny material accentuating the roundness of her belly, her hair a pile of curls on top of her head. She looked pointedly at the blonde—who did a high kick and a fancy turn—then raised an eyebrow at Brady as if to say, *You'd better have a good explanation for this one, buddy.*

"Oops," Matt murmured.

But Brady didn't seem worried. He just brushed past his brother, limped to the door, took hold of J.C.'s face and kissed her as if he was a dying man and she was his last chance at salvation. She sagged against him, her hands on his shoulders. Applause broke out, broken by a few catcalls. The two finally came up for air. J.C.'s cheeks were flushed but Brady just looked…content.

Matt didn't understand it but that didn't mean he couldn't be glad for his brother.

Brady grabbed J.C.'s hand, gave everyone in the room a wave and tugged her out the door.

After the happy couple took off, the rest of the women came into the room. He recognized a few from town, raised a hand in greeting to Mary Susan Gallagher, an old high school classmate. But when Mary Susan stepped to the side and another woman came into view, he froze.

Connie.

Their eyes clashed. Held. She looked…different. Her hair was spikier than usual on top, the sides slicked back, showcasing her long neck and the sparkle of her dangling earrings. The dark jeans and deep green top she wore hinted at curves where before he could've sworn there were only angles. His fingers curled into his palms, he let his gaze roam from the top of her head down to the pointy-toed black boots with three-inch heels that made her legs seem endless.

And for a moment, one dark, unbidden second in time, he wondered what it would be like to have those legs wrapped around him.

Desire lashed through him, quick and sharp as a whip. And then she started toward him with her long-limbed stride, her hips swaying subtly.

She stopped a mere foot away. Close enough for her surprisingly sexy scent to reach him.

"If they weren't so great together," she said, jerking a thumb over her shoulder to where Brady and J.C. had retreated, "they'd be nauseating." Then she smiled at him, a tremulous smile that was as unlike her as the smoky eye makeup and slash of shiny color on her mouth. "This seat taken?" she asked, patting the empty stool to his left.

He figured she'd avoid him after the way they'd left things last night. He'd purposely kept his distance from her today at work, choosing to start the pruning on the next block of vines rather than torturing himself by being near her all day.

And yet, here she was, asking if she could sit next to him. An edginess in her blue eyes, her fingers worrying the strap of her purse at her shoulder. Interesting.

She was interesting. And sexier in those damn tight jeans and top than he was comfortable with.

Reminding himself she was Connie, just Connie, a woman he'd known more than half his life, he pulled the stool out. "Please. Can I get you a drink?"

"No. Thanks. What I'd really love is some food." She waved the bartender over then leaned forward, her elbows resting on the counter, her butt lifted off the chair. Matt's mouth went dry and he jerked his gaze away. "Is the kitchen still open?" she asked.

"Bar menu's available until closing time," the guy said, handing Connie a one-sided, laminated menu.

"Thank God," she murmured, sitting back as she scanned the menu. "I'm starving."

"I'd offer you some appetizers but I think we've been cleaned out," Matt said. He leaned against the bar. "You were with J.C.?"

She nodded. "They called me a few hours ago—well, Liz did—said they were throwing J.C. an impromptu bachelorette party, and since the girls are spending the weekend at their father's, I figured why not?" The bartender came back and Connie placed her order for a cheeseburger and fries. She glanced at Matt. "We were at The County Line when someone suggested we come over here and crash the stag party. I don't think any of us thought we'd lose both guests of honor."

"Things were winding down here, anyway." He shifted to look out at the room. The dancer had put her military costume back on and was gathering her sound equipment while most of the guests—both male and female—started making their way out the door. Aidan stood in deep conversation with their cousin, David.

"So," Connie said, turning slightly in her seat to face him. "How'd the party go? Anything wild happen? Any *Hangover* moments?"

He grinned, appreciating her reference to the movie. "No tigers or babies have been spotted and as far as I know, everyone still has all of their teeth."

"As long as the groom does, that's all that matters." The bartender set a glass of ice water in front of her and Connie smiled her thanks. "Look, about last night—"

"Are you going to apologize?"

Her pretty mouth thinned. "For putting an arrogant man in his place? Can't say I've ever regretted that," she told him, reminding him of his words when he'd asked if he should apologize for kissing her.

"So you're obviously not here to beg my forgiveness. Did you come over expecting me to apologize?"

Brushing her short bangs to the side, she stared down at her water. His own fingers twitched with the need to touch her hair. To see if it was as soft as he imagined.

"I came over because…" She stirred the ice in her glass with her straw then abruptly let go and met his eyes. "I came over because you looked…alone."

"Hard to be alone when I'm surrounded by people."

"Okay," she said slowly. "Maybe alone wasn't the right word. More like…lonely."

The muscles in his shoulders tensed but he didn't move. Couldn't. Not when his breath was locked in his chest. Not when he was afraid she was right.

Still, he forced a grin. "Not lonely," he assured her as he deliberately slid his gaze down her figure. "But glad for the company anyway."

DISAPPOINTMENT SETTLED COLD and heavy in Connie's chest at Matt's blatant flirtatious behavior. What had she expected, that he'd open up to her? That he'd be glad she'd noticed how unhappy he'd seemed sitting at the bar by himself? God, even in a room filled with people he kept himself separate.

She wondered if he realized he did it. If he understood why.

Taking a drink, she shook her head slightly. Not her problem. If Matt wanted to isolate himself from his family and friends and everyone in Jewell, that was up to him. And ultimately would be his loss.

"I'm sure if you played your cards right and spewed some of that stilted charm the stripper's way—"

"Exotic dancer," he said with a grin.

"You would have company all night."

"Your faith in my ability to pick up strange women in bars is heartwarming."

What could she do? She laughed. "Well, as I mentioned last night, you're awful pretty."

She didn't doubt there were plenty of women right here at The Empire who'd happily throw away their inhibitions, common sense and morals for the chance to spend a night in his bed. Especially looking like he did now in a pair of jeans and a gray V-neck sweater that accentuated the broadness of his shoulders, clung to the hard plane of his chest. His long hair was loose and he was smiling down at her, his head inclined just so.

And as he held her gaze captive with his, she had the feeling there was more to him than she could read in the depths of his green eyes. More than he let anyone see.

For the space of one heartbeat, she wanted to be the person he let in. The one he showed his true self to.

"How's your mom doing?" she asked, needing to get them back on equal footing. Or maybe she just needed to regain her own equilibrium. Either way, his smile faded, his eyes cooled.

"Far as I know she's fine."

The bartender set Connie's food in front of her.

"Thanks," she told him before squirting ketchup next to her fries. "J.C. said they invited her to come out with us all tonight but she claimed she was too tired." She dipped a fry in ketchup, bit into it. "Did she seem okay at the rehearsal?"

His shrug was irritable. "I guess." He helped himself to a fry. "Why?"

"I'm worried about her." Connie took the pickles off her burger and replaced the top bun. "I think she's upset about the wedding."

He frowned. "She may not have been thrilled with how things started between J.C. and Brady—"

"No. Not like that. I mean…I think she's just missing your dad. Wishing he could be here for it."

His expression blanked. "I'm sure she is. But she's strong. She'll get through. Besides, she has Al now."

A couple of the guests waved and said their goodbyes as they walked past the bar. Matt stood long enough to shake hands and thank them for coming. Connie waited until he'd sat back down before speaking again.

"Do you think," she said slowly, voicing an idea she'd been wondering a lot about, "that part of the reason Diane did this whole thing with you and your brothers is because she feels guilty for being with Al?"

He grimaced, as if the thought of his mother being with a man other than his father was on par with waterboarding in his mind. But when he spoke, his voice was mild. "Did she tell you that?"

"No. It's just…" She wiped her mouth with a napkin. "I saw how devastated she was by Tom's death. How lonely she was without him. And when I remember how much they loved each other, it just makes me think that she might feel a bit guilty about moving on with her life."

His eyes narrowed. "And the best way to assuage that guilt would be to make his greatest dream come true."

"It's just a thought," she said. A thought she hadn't been able to get out of her mind. No, she couldn't imagine that a woman who'd loved her husband as much as Diane had loved Tom would be able to just marry someone else without some sort of emotional consequence.

That was the thing about unconditional love. It could kick your ass if you weren't careful.

"Either way," Matt said bitterly, "I'm sure wherever the old man is now, he's kicking up his heels. He's finally gotten his way."

Her appetite gone, she set the remnants of her burger down. When he looked at it then raised his brows at her, she pushed the plate toward him. "He used to talk about you, you know. Your dad," she added, then mentally rolled her eyes because of course he knew who she meant. "He followed your career. Used to brag to me about you." Though she sensed Matt's tension, his anger, she pushed on. "He was proud of you."

He leaned toward her, so close she could see amber flecks in his eyes. "Don't."

Forcing herself not to shrink away, she licked her lips. His eyes followed the movement. Heated. "Don't what?"

"Don't try and fix things between me and a dead man. It's too late."

She laid her hand on his wrist. His skin was warm, the hair on his arm coarse. "I'm sorry."

He slid his arm out from under her fingers. "I'm not. It's all in the past. I'd much rather focus on the present. Or better yet, the future. Preferably the future of the Diamond Dust."

She wrinkled her nose in surprise. "Because suddenly you're on board with wanting to be a part of it?"

"Because I want to make sure the Diamond Dust grows. That we produce high-quality, award-winning wines."

A suspicion formed in the back of her mind. "Right. And if the Diamond Dust grows," she said, watching him carefully, "if the wines get recognition, then so do you. Your reputation as an up-and-coming winemaker would remain intact. It might even improve, especially if you can help establish the Diamond Dust as a top winery."

He didn't so much as blink. "Would that be so bad?"

She bit her lower lip. No, of course that wouldn't be bad. And she couldn't blame him for wanting to continue to make the most of his career, even if he was using the Diamond Dust to do so. If the winery benefitted as well, what did it matter if Matt's main priority was his own personal agenda?

"I just…I can't help but wonder," she said, "if this really is about the Diamond Dust, about helping your career. Or if it's personal."

"IT'S NOT," MATT SAID shortly, suddenly wishing he'd stuck with beer. Or even something harder.

Connie slid to the edge of her stool and crossed her legs as she leaned forward. "I think it is. You're trying to prove yourself to your dad, aren't you?"

Her words, though spoken softly, hit him like a fist to the jaw. He curled his fingers into his thighs but kept his expression neutral. "I hadn't realized running a vineyard made you an expert on psychology."

She flushed, color washing over her cheeks, and damned if it didn't suit her. "I don't need to be an expert to know you and Tom had some…issues."

"My mom called it a personality conflict," he said easily, though remembering the never-ending arguments, how disappointed his father had always been still made his stomach cramp.

The same rush of emotions that he'd experienced as a cocky teenager washed over him. Anger. Resentment. Love. And the hope that someday he'd be able to make the old man proud. The more control Tom tried to exert over Matt's life, the harder he'd pulled away. And when he thought he'd finally gotten free, his father had somehow managed to yank him back under his thumb. Even from the grave the old man was holding his leash.

He just hoped he lasted the year without the damn thing choking the life from him.

"Listen," Connie said, lowering her voice, "I, more than anyone, can understand what it was like for you. Butting heads with your father the way you used to."

He almost laughed. Yes, they'd butted heads. Usually because both of them had run full steam at the other, more than ready to prove themselves right. And, more importantly, show the other he was wrong.

The hell with water. He ordered a beer. "We clashed," he told Connie. "But it was a long time ago."

"That's the thing, though—it doesn't matter how long ago it happened," she said with a sigh, her shoulders rounded, her hands clasped in her lap. "Some things always have the power to cut you off at the knees."

Because he knew she was speaking from personal experience and because he hated the sadness, the resignation in her tone, he laid his hand over hers. She startled but didn't pull away. "They only have power if we give it to them."

Her lips quirked. "Now who's being the psychoanalyst?"

"I wasn't analyzing you," he said, unable to stop himself from brushing his thumb back and forth across her soft skin. "I was just giving you advice. Damn good advice, too. I highly recommend you take it."

She laughed, the sound washing over him like a cool breeze on a hot day. "How about I just promise to keep it in mind?"

He smiled. "Why don't we get out of here?" he heard himself say, surprised by the words but more surprised by how much he meant them. "We could grab a bite to eat—"

"I just ate," she pointed out, looking at him as if he'd just suggested they run off to Las Vegas for an all-night buffet.

"Right." Damn. He needed to get a grip. It was just Connie. All he wanted was to go somewhere they could talk. He liked talking with her. Liked listening to her. Even when she was probing wounds better left scabbed over. "How about coffee?" He frowned. That was, if they could find a coffee place that was still open at midnight. "Or—"

"I paid Mona."

Shit.

Clenching his teeth, Matt glanced at Aidan. He was so busy glaring at his brother, it took him a moment to realize he'd tightened his hold on Connie's hand. And that she was trying to tug free of him.

He let go. Took a long drink of his beer. "Thanks."

"Don't thank me," Aidan said. "You owe me five hundred dollars."

Good thing he'd already swallowed his drink or he'd have choked.

"Five hundred dollars?" Connie asked. "For the stripper?"

"Exotic dancer," Matt corrected automatically.

She whistled. "Maybe I should take up dancing. Exotically, that is."

He grinned and winked at her. "Sugar, I'm sure you'd be a natural."

She gave him a look that said he was full of shit while Aidan's gaze narrowed.

"I'm heading out," Aidan said. "Connie, do you need a ride?"

Wait. What was this? He set his beer down. "You didn't drive?"

She shook her head. "Liz picked me up, but since she went home from The County Line, I rode over here with one of J.C.'s bridesmaids." She slid to her feet, bringing them eye to eye, her thigh brushing his knee. Their eyes held for one long beat before she turned to his brother. "I'd love a ride home, Aidan. Thanks."

And she smiled, more at ease with Aidan than she'd ever been with Matt.

Not that it bugged him. Much.

"Let's go, then," Aidan said, helping Connie on with her coat. "See you tomorrow," he said to Matt.

Matt nodded. As they left, he sipped his beer. He'd never been one to want to follow in someone else's footsteps. He preferred making his own way.

But as he watched his brother and Connie walk away, Aidan's hand on the small of her back, watched her laugh at something his brother said, Matt wished, for the first time in his life, that he was in Aidan's shoes.

CHAPTER TEN

"I HAVEN'T HEARD THIS song in forever," Connie said as "Breathe" came on the radio. Sitting in the passenger seat of Aidan's car as they left the bar, she turned up the sound and started singing along. Softly, yes, but the sounds she emitted were wobbly, way off-key and an affront to music lovers everywhere.

He winced and pressed his ear against his shoulder in an attempt to muffle the sound. "Who sings this song?"

She glanced at him. "Faith Hill."

"Well then, how about we let her sing it? Alone."

"That hurts."

He pulled to a stop at the intersection of Colonial Heights and Bolivar Drive. "Not any worse than the brush burns you'll get if you don't stop singing and I shove you out of the car."

"Will you at least slow down first?"

"Depends if you try to hit any high notes or not."

"I appreciate that."

They shared a smile but hers quickly faded and she averted her eyes. He'd had the feeling something was off between them lately. Ever since she'd found out he, Brady and Matt were going to be taking over the Diamond Dust, she'd avoided him as much as possible. And when it wasn't possible, she'd been distant. Cool. Reserved.

But he didn't have time to worry about that now. Not when there was another concern niggling at him. Because there was no traffic, and he wanted to see her face when he asked, he turned the radio off, kept his foot on the brake. His eyes on her profile.

"Is there something going on between you and Matt I should know about?"

She blinked, her mouth dropping open. And even in the harsh glow of the streetlight, he could see color stain her cheeks.

The beginning of a headache started behind his left eye. Matt and Connie were not, in his opinion, a good combination. Not for them or him.

"Now, don't be jealous," she said with a light laugh. But he'd known her long enough, was close enough to her to realize it was fake. "You know you're my A-Number-One Favorite Sheppard."

"Really? Then why have you been avoiding me?"

She looked out the window. "I've just been busy. It's not personal."

"Okay," he said slowly, feeling there was more going on than what she was saying. He eased his foot off the brake and turned right. "But you didn't answer my question."

Connie wasn't the type for games. Things with her

were either black or white. When she was happy, she showed it. And when she was upset? Watch out.

Which was why he hated this evasiveness, these undercurrents he couldn't define.

He much preferred knowing where he stood with someone.

"If you're asking me if there's something sexual going on between us, the answer is no. I mean, let's get serious here. Can you picture Matt and me together?"

"No. I can't. Which is why I asked."

Connie was stable. Settled. She had two little girls and a mentally ill mother to care for. She was as dependable as the sun rising in the east while Matt was… Matt. No matter how lush the yard, he always thought the grass was greener next door.

She was all about family, about loyalty. Matt was all about himself.

"You two seemed cozy at the bar," he said.

"We were just talking, Dad. I swear." And though he couldn't see her, he knew she was rolling her eyes at him.

"I guess I hadn't realized you two had that much in common. Enough for a deep conversation."

Enough for them to have been practically holding hands when Aidan joined them.

"We were talking about your dad," she said tightly, her arms crossed over her chest.

And if he kept pushing her, she'd take his head off and toss it out the window.

He wanted, badly, to hear the answer he was looking

for. That she wasn't interested in Matt, not now, not ever. That the little scene he'd witnessed between them wouldn't turn into something…sexual…eventually.

It wasn't that he had anything against Matt and Connie getting together. He just knew it wouldn't work. Why go through the hassle when things would only end badly?

And when they did, he'd be the one stuck cleaning up the mess.

They drove in silence for a few minutes. When he made a left onto her street, she shifted in her seat to face him. "You bringing someone to the wedding?" she asked almost reluctantly, as if she didn't really want to have a conversation but didn't want to sit in silence any longer, either.

"Marlene Lucca."

"Marlene, huh? Must be serious between you two."

"Now who's jealous?"

"Yes," she said dryly, "I'm absolutely green with it. I'm just curious as to your intentions toward this woman. After all, you've been seeing each other for a year—"

"It's only been eight months."

She waved that away. "Yeah, but you're bringing her to your brother's wedding where your entire family will be in attendance. That's a big deal. Especially to a woman."

He pulled to a stop behind her minivan in the driveway. "Are you trying to get back at me for asking about you and Matt?"

"Not at all." She unbuckled her seat belt. "I'll bide my time until you least expect it and then I'll get back at you for your…interest in my love life. Or in this case, lack thereof."

Instead of waiting for him, she opened the door and climbed out. He did the same, standing by the back corner of the car, hand held out for her keys. "I'll be sure to watch my back."

"See that you do," she said, dropping the keys into his open palm. "And I'm glad you're bringing Marlene tomorrow. She's a lot better than the last woman you brought to the Diamond Dust."

He clenched the keys, the sharp edges digging into his skin. He hadn't brought any woman home in eight years. Not since he and Yvonne had moved there when his father got sick. Eight years and Connie's dislike of his ex-wife hadn't waned. Yvonne could come across as cold and snobbish, especially when she was nervous. And for some reason, she'd always been nervous around Connie.

Other than nerves, he'd never been certain of Yvonne's feelings toward Connie. If she'd held any animosity, she'd never let on.

Story of his marriage. He'd never known what his wife was thinking.

"How about we make a pact," he said, unlocking the door for Connie and handing her back the keys. "We won't discuss our love lives—past, present, future or lack thereof—ever again?"

She thrust her hand out. "Deal." Opening the door, she gave him a smart-ass grin. "But if I was to say something about it, I'd say that I like Marlene. She's very nice."

He made a noncommittal sound. Really, what was there to say? Marlene was nice. She was also beautiful, ran a successful accounting service and was a gourmet cook. But in spite of her stellar qualities, Aidan wasn't looking for anything serious. A fact he'd made clear from the beginning.

One marriage per lifetime was his limit.

He hoped, for Connie's sake, it was hers, too.

"Hey," he heard himself say, stopping her as she stepped inside. "Are we okay?"

Even in the dim light he could see her back go rigid. "Why wouldn't we be?"

"You tell me."

He didn't think she would, but then she wiped her palms down the front of her jeans before clasping her hands in front of her. "You didn't fight for me."

"I'm not following..."

"I've been a part of the Diamond Dust for sixteen years, and though your mother's name may be listed as owner, we both know you and I were the ones who've kept it running since your dad died. And yet, as soon as your brothers came back into the picture, you didn't even think twice about pushing me aside."

"That's not true," he said. "No one is pushing you aside. There's room for all of us at the winery."

"Yeah, well, I guess we'll see about that, won't we?" She started to shut the door but stopped and met his eyes. "As far as you and I being okay…I want us to be," she said so softly he had to lean in to hear her. "But I don't know if that's possible."

SHE WASN'T LATE, CONNIE assured herself as she glanced at her watch then reached back into the minivan for the three bags of groceries. It was barely five and Brady and J.C.'s wedding didn't start for another hour so she had plenty of time. She shouldn't have slept in this morning, should have gotten up and taken care of her errands before noon, but she'd had a restless night thanks to her racing thoughts.

She'd turned her conversation with Matt over and over in her mind. Wondering if she'd imagined the way he'd looked at her. As if he found her interesting. Attractive.

As if he was attracted to her.

She shook her head and shut the driver's side door. Sure, he'd kissed her that night on his mother's porch but that had been…well, it had been amazing. But nothing close to that had happened between them since.

Carefully making her way up her mother's uneven cement sidewalk in her high heels, she adjusted her grip on the heavy bags. That heated look in his eyes last night couldn't have been real. The sparks arcing between them. She and Matt were…well…not friends, but trying to be. And once the paperwork went through for the partnership, he'd be her boss. End of story.

And a really good excuse for her to keep her distance from him. At least personally.

The crisp, evening air stung her nose as she climbed the steps to her mother's small, ranch-style house. A branch from the large elm tree swayed in the breeze, tapping against the side of the house. Though the temperatures were dropping, the sky was clear, the setting sun a blending of pinks and peach. It was a perfect winter evening for a wedding.

And if she wanted to be there in time to see the bride walk down the makeshift aisle in the middle of Diane's living room, she'd better get a move on. Planning on staying only long enough to drop off her mother's groceries, Connie knocked on the front door.

When no one answered her second knock, she tried the knob, turning it easily in her hand. She opened the door.

And stepped into chaos.

Connie's stomach pitched. *No. No, please, not today.*

But, as usual when dealing with her mother, her prayers went unanswered. Dread filled her, told her to turn around and get out while she still could. Reminded her that she'd already spent a lifetime caring for her mother and nothing changed. It would never change.

And yet she couldn't walk away. This was her mother, for God's sake. Margaret had never been an ideal mother, had never given Connie the care, the love, she'd craved. Whether that was due to her illness or some other reason, Connie wasn't sure. All she knew was that in the end, the whys didn't matter. Her mother needed her.

She shut the door behind her.

The room was in shadows, the blinds drawn tight, but there was enough light to see the place was trashed. Dirty dishes, glasses, bags of chips and crackers and all manner of garbage covered every available surface, from the end tables to the couch to her mother's favorite chair. Papers, magazines and unopened mail were piled on the coffee table. Hard to believe so much destruction could've been done since she was last there two days ago. Then again, she'd once witnessed her mother destroy a room in a single afternoon.

The TV in the corner was on, a gossip show flashing across the screen. The volume loud, the sound echoed in Connie's ears, intensifying the pounding in her head.

Sidestepping an overturned laundry basket and pile of clothes—only God knew if they were clean or dirty— she crossed the room and shut off the T.V.

"Mom?" she said into the sudden silence. "Mom, it's me."

A loud crash sounded and she jumped, whirling in the direction of the noise. Realizing it came from the kitchen, she hurried down the hall then skidded to a stop in the doorway. She gave a cry, as if she'd been punched in the stomach. Her eyes widened at the shards of her grandmother's antique china set littering the floor.

But that wasn't the worst part. Oh, no, not by a long shot. The worst part was that her mother was standing next to the counter in a stained nightgown, her blue eyes wild, her feet bare, her graying brown hair hanging limp and dirty to her shoulders.

Connie swallowed her rising panic as she took a hesitant step into the kitchen. "Mom?"

Margaret's head came up like that of a wild animal sensing danger. She blinked, her eyes coming into focus. Then she picked up a plate from a pile on the counter, used both hands to lift it over her head and smashed it to the floor.

Connie winced. "What are you doing?" She tossed the bags of groceries onto the table, slipped and had to catch her balance by grabbing on to a chair.

"I was going to make myself some toast," Margaret said, her tone eerily calm, her voice hoarse, as if she'd been screaming nonstop for days. "I went to get a plate for it and I noticed this—" She held up another plate from the set of white china with delicate, hand-painted pink roses and waved it around. "I've always hated this pattern," she said. "It was my father's mother's but I wanted my maternal grandmother's dishes." Her lips formed a pout. "I wanted the pretty ones. But my mother gave them to my sister instead."

She lobbed the plate across the room but her throw didn't have enough strength behind it and the plate hit a cabinet door with a dull thud.

Before her mother could pick up any more ammunition, Connie grabbed both of her arms. "Stop!" She shook her lightly until Margaret met her eyes. "Stop this right now."

God, she should've known not to relax. Should've known something like this was bound to happen. It'd been months since her mother's last episode. Months of dealing with Margaret's usual cries for attention. Her neediness. But there had been no mood swings, no days of mania followed by weeks of depression so bad she couldn't get out of bed.

She should've known—had known—that the relative normalcy wouldn't last.

"What do you care what I do?" Margaret asked, her face crumpling as tears flowed down her cheeks. "All you care about is yourself. Do you ever think of me? Think of what I go through? No," she sobbed, her thin shoulders shaking. "You're too busy with your own life. Too busy for me."

A lump formed in Connie's throat but she refused to cry. "You know that's not true. And look, I'm right here."

"You don't understand," Margaret whispered hoarsely. "You don't know what it's like to have a child so…so… unconcerned for her own mother's needs."

Connie rubbed at the headache pulsing at her temples. "You look…" Haggard. Ill. And she smelled as if she hadn't bathed in days. "Tired. Have you eaten anything besides toast today?"

Margaret sniffed, wiped her red-tipped nose with a paper towel. "I couldn't eat. All those horrible memories of my mother. Of how cruel she was to me. How she always favored your Aunt Barb…"

Horrible. Right. Like mother like daughter. Connie was fairly certain her grandmother had suffered from the same mental disorder as Margaret, though she'd gone her entire lifetime undiagnosed and untreated.

Unlike her daughter, who *forgot* to take her medicine.

"Why don't I make you something to eat," Connie said soothingly, "while you take a shower?"

Knowing her mother's manic moods, she figured Margaret had been living on nothing but coffee and, if she had to hazard a guess, possibly scotch for the past few days.

Damn. She'd sensed the building of a manic phase when her mother had gone to the E.R. but she'd convinced herself Margaret was just being Margaret. Wanting, needing attention and doing whatever she could to get it. Even if it meant saying she was having chest pains.

Her throat closed. She'd been desperate to keep the peace between them, to prolong the sense that everything was fine, and in the end she'd been blindsided by the harsh reality of her mother's illness.

"Did you get my groceries?" Margaret asked, her voice wobbly.

"Yes." Didn't she always get her groceries on Saturday?

"What about English muffins? You know I like an English muffin for breakfast."

Instead of answering, Connie simply dug through the bags, found the package of English muffins and held them up. She always did what her mother asked, she thought dully. Had spent her entire life trying to make her happy, trying to appease her. Trying to make her okay.

"I'd like an English muffin and some scrambled eggs and bacon," Margaret said, her fingers tearing at the paper towel. Pieces of it floated to the floor. Her mouth turned down. "What are you wearing?"

Connie glanced down at her red dress. "It's Brady and J.C.'s wedding today. Remember? I told you last night on the phone?"

"You're leaving me?" Margaret wailed, her face white.

"I'm not leaving." Not until she'd made sure her mother was calm. That she was safe.

"You'll...you'll still be here when I get out of the shower?" she persisted, fresh tears falling. "You'll take care of me?"

Connie's own eyes stung, her throat burned. Even when she was a child, their roles had been reversed. She'd been the one who'd given her mother the love and attention she craved. Had taken on the responsibility of making sure their home was clean. That meals were prepared. And when Margaret's illness overtook her, it was Connie who cleaned up the mess when she went into a manic phase. Who sat by her mother's bedside when depression all but crippled her.

"Yes," she managed to say, love and guilt and the weight of her responsibility pressing down on her. Stopping her from leaving. "I'll take care of you."

"I'VE BEEN LOOKING ALL over for you," Aidan said as he stood in the doorway to his empty office. "I thought you took off."

More like expected him to, Matt thought. Sitting in his brother's seat, his feet up on his desk, a full plate of food on his stomach, he shrugged. "You must not have been looking very hard since I've been right here."

"Everyone else is downstairs."

He took a bite of a spring roll. Chewed and swallowed. "Which is why I'm right here."

Not that he had anything against wedding receptions. Or parties in general. But word of his less-than-triumphant return to the Diamond Dust had quickly spread and he'd gotten tired of trying to act like giving up his freedom because of his mother's extortion was a good thing.

"Come on," Aidan said. "The photographer wants to get a few more pictures."

"He took at least a dozen right after the ceremony."

"Those had everyone in them. He wants to take a few of just our family now."

Biting back a sigh, Matt got up and walked with his brother down the hall to the stairs. As they descended, the sounds of the party grew louder. Laughter and conversation mixed with the quartet playing in the background, the gentle clang of silver on dishes. When they reached the foyer, Matt glanced into the living room. The chairs that had been set up in rows for the ceremony with military precision now surrounded several round tables in both that room and the connecting dining room. Most of the fifty or so guests were still eating but a few had gotten up to mingle or refill their plates from the buffet table being watched over by the caterers J.C.'s family had brought in all the way from Virginia Beach.

"You might want to straighten your tie," Aidan said before he turned and headed toward the family room.

Matt glanced in the mirror on the wall. Huh. His tie was crooked. Must've happened when he'd loosened it before he'd started eating. Setting his plate on the small table next to the wall, he fixed his tie, combed both hands through his hair and then picked up his plate again.

Once in the family room, he stepped up next to Aidan, who, as usual, looked perfectly pressed in his suit, not a single hair brave enough to be out of place.

The photographer was taking shots of J.C., Brady and Diane in front of the fireplace. It, too, had been decorated for the festivities with flowers and lit candles on the mantel and larger bouquets on each side. Al stood nearby looking regal with his silver hair and politician's smile.

As he watched, Al winked at Diane. Her expression warmed as their gazes held. Matt shifted uncomfortably. It was one thing to know his mother was marrying another man. It was another to witness their affection for each other firsthand.

Do you think that part of the reason Diane did this whole thing with you and your brothers is because she feels guilty for being with Al?

He had to admit, until Connie had asked him that question, he'd been certain the only reason his mother was forcing him back to the Diamond Dust was because of his father. But now he had to consider the possibility that his mother was using them all in some off-the-wall attempt to assuage her guilt so she could remarry with a clear conscience.

And did that make this whole crappy situation better? Or worse?

The sound of J.C.'s laugh rose above the crowd. He didn't know if it was the pregnancy or the wedding band on her finger, but J.C. positively glowed in a gown of a subtle rose shade that left lots of neck and shoulder exposed but managed to flow over her belly without clinging. Brady couldn't take his eyes off his wife and at one point Matt could've sworn his brother had actually smiled.

Seemed it was truly a miraculous day.

And while there were plenty of people he knew, relatives and old friends he hadn't seen in years, he found himself searching out one particular person. But he had yet to see her.

Handing his empty plate to a passing waiter, he couldn't stop himself from asking Aidan, "Where's Connie?"

Aidan slid him a dismissive glance. "Not here."

"I can see that," Matt said, fighting to keep his cool. Not easy when Aidan was so damned good at pushing his buttons. "I was just wondering if you'd heard from her. It's not like her to just not show up like this."

"How do you know what it is or isn't like Connie to do?"

He drummed his fingers against his thigh. "I've known her since I was a kid."

"I haven't heard from her," Aidan admitted grudgingly. "If she doesn't get here soon, I'll call. In the meantime, remember this, you are not, under any circumstances, to start sniffing around Connie. You understand me?"

Matt narrowed his eyes. "Since when has what you told me to do—or in this case, not do—ever stopped me?"

Aidan edged closer to his brother so they were toe-to-toe. "She's not like the women you usually hook up with."

"I'm not hooking up with her. I just asked if you'd seen her."

"Boys," their mother called. "We're ready for you."

They both turned toward her. She wasn't fooling anyone with that faux cheery tone, Matt thought. He'd heard the sharpness underneath it. Seen the faint, disapproving frown pinching her forehead. The look in her eye that clearly said if they didn't knock it off she'd knock their heads together.

The photographer arranged them in front of the

fireplace. J.C. and Brady in the middle, leaning toward each other. Diane and Al to J.C.'s right. Aidan and Matt next to Brady.

One big happy family.

So why did he feel separate from it all? He traveled so often, was away for such long periods of time that when he did come home he often felt like a stranger. Disconnected.

An outsider.

A flash of red caught his eye as someone entered the kitchen through the French doors. He stilled, his camera-ready smile sliding off his face as his breath froze in his chest. Connie. In a shiny red, low-cut dress that ended above the knees, her hair dark and spiky around her angular face, her feet encased in a pair of strappy high heels.

She was beautiful.

He frowned. No. This was Connie. She was many things. Smart. Funny. Even sexy. Yeah, he could deal with all those. But he couldn't deal with thinking she was anything more. Didn't want her to be beautiful to him. His mind was already messed up enough with crazy thoughts about her. About kissing her. Touching her.

"How about some smiles?" the photographer asked. And even though the guy was behind his camera lens, Matt knew he was talking to him.

He looked back at the camera and smiled while the picture was taken. Then he searched out Connie again. But this time when he saw her, he was almost cut off at the knees at the stark look of longing on her face as she stared at them. The desperation. And sadness.

He stepped forward, not really knowing his intentions, only that he wanted to get to her. But as he moved, the photographer snapped another picture.

"Oops," the guy said. "Let's not run off yet. Just a few more and then you'll be free to go."

Feeling the weight of his family's curious stares, Matt ground out the facsimile of a smile. "Sorry."

They were rearranged, this time with J.C. and Diane in the center and the men around them. When Matt looked for Connie, she was no longer there. Fighting his agitation to just be done already, he stood where he was told and smiled on cue for the next ten minutes. After the last shot had been taken—this one of just Aidan, Brady and Matt—he took off. A quick search of the kitchen, living and dining rooms proved fruitless.

Where the hell had she gone?

Feeling a sense of loss that he wouldn't get to see her again tonight, he went back to the kitchen. People pressed on either side of him, smiling, laughing. His breath lodged in his chest, his thoughts tumbled around in his head. Needing a breather, he slid out onto the back patio through the French doors. The wind blew his hair into his face. He shoved it back and stretched his arms overhead as he inhaled deeply.

This was better. Just him and the quiet. The dark. No questions. No curious looks. No expectations.

No weird sense of longing. Of feeling as if maybe,

just maybe, by keeping his family at a distance, he was missing out on something.

He lowered his arms. The thought of rejoining the reception had sweat breaking out along his lower back despite the cold temperature. But he had no choice. Not if he wanted to see if Connie was still around.

He turned to go back inside when a voice stopped him.

"All done hiding out?"

CHAPTER ELEVEN

MATT TURNED TOWARD THE sound of that chiding voice. Raised his eyebrows at the sight of Connie sitting in the shadows, a half glass of wine in her hand, an open bottle on the table in front of her. His heart stuttered. He'd never seen her look so sad. So...alone.

"Excuse me?" he asked, trying to wrap his mind around why she was sitting outside in the cold by herself.

And why he was so damned glad to see her.

"I asked if you were through hiding out here?"

"I wasn't hiding. I was...regrouping. What about you?"

Lights from the house spilled through the kitchen window, casting her face in shadow. Still, he clearly saw the wry look she sent him. "Yeah, sure," she said, taking a long drink of wine. "I'm doing the regrouping thing, too."

He shifted. Told himself not to ask. That her sitting out here by herself wasn't his concern. That he didn't need to know what had put the sorrow in her eyes.

"You okay?" he asked, wincing at the question and the harshness of his tone.

She lifted her glass in a mock salute. "Just dandy."

Good. That was…good. He shoved his hands into his pockets. Took them out then dropped onto the chair next to her. "We missed you at the wedding," he said, hoping to get some insight into what the hell was going on with her.

"Something came up." She was silent a moment, then asked, "How was it?"

"It was a wedding. Aidan didn't lose the rings, the bride's family didn't object and Brady managed to say 'I do' without making it sound like a growl. I'd say it was a success."

She frowned into her wine. "I always thought the Diamond Dust should host weddings. It's the perfect place for it."

True. And plenty of wineries hosted weddings and other special events. They had the space, and extra income was always welcome, but it'd take time and effort to get something like that up and running. Would make the winery more of a tourist destination than a place to get complex, quality wine, and that wasn't what he wanted for the business.

He scowled down at the table. Hell. Now he was starting to think in terms of what he did and didn't want for his father's company. As if he actually planned on sticking it out past a year. It was his own personal nightmare.

"The Diamond Dust is a winery," he told her. "Anything else would take away from its main purpose."

Her head tilted to the side, her chin propped on her

fist, Connie studied him. "You know, that's just what Aidan would say."

He jerked back as if she'd slapped him. "Well for God's sake, don't tell him I agree with him or he may just change his mind out of spite."

When she didn't acknowledge his lame attempt at humor with so much as a roll of her midnight blue eyes, he wondered if he'd misjudged her sobriety. He leaned forward and studied her. Her eyes seemed clear enough, her speech steady. He lifted the bottle of wine, estimated there were at least two glasses missing from it then slid it out of her reach.

"What say we go inside?" he asked as he stood. He kept his voice calm. She may not be drunk but there was an edginess to her that told him to tread with caution. "We'll get you something to eat. You can say hello to the happy couple."

"I don't want to go inside," she said petulantly. "And I don't need you out here pretending to be nice."

He gave her his most charming smile. "Sugar, I am nice."

She snorted. Took another drink of wine. "You're a real prince. And you're getting everything I ever wanted. But the real kicker is," she bit out, "you *don't* want it."

He narrowed his eyes. Sat back. "I realize I'm late to your little one-lady party here, but I have no idea what you're talking about."

"Doesn't matter," she muttered.

If that was true he'd shave his head. "Come on," he

said, tugging lightly at her arm to help her up. She pulled away from him.

"I need…I need a few more minutes out here. Some time to clear my head before I…I have to face everyone."

"Clear your head about what?"

But she just shrugged and averted her eyes. Something was going on with her. And while he could probably find out if he let her finish that bottle of wine, he didn't work that way. Contrary to his family's beliefs, he didn't always take the easy way out.

"All right," he said slowly as he took off his suit coat. "If that's how you want to do this."

And he draped his coat over her shoulders, picked up the wine and went back inside.

CONNIE'S EYES STUNG. From the cold. Not because Matt had just left her out here alone.

Worse than that, he'd taken her wine.

Probably a good thing, she admitted with a sigh as she set her glass aside. Her head was still pounding from dealing with her mother. And as for her being alone… that was exactly what she wanted right now. She couldn't go inside. Not after witnessing the Sheppards getting their picture taken together.

A stupid thing to get upset about, but sometimes emotions didn't make sense. Which was why, when she'd seen them standing there close together, smiles on their faces, the truth had hit her like a slap. No matter how hard Connie might try, no matter how much she pretended otherwise, she wasn't part of their family.

And wishing for things to be different was just plain pathetic.

She was an employee. A friend. Someone they could count on. Someone they valued for her dedication and loyalty to the Diamond Dust. She was Tom's pet project. The little lost girl he'd brought into their lives. He'd shown her how to make something of herself. How to be more than just her mother's daughter. More than her mother's caretaker.

He'd been the one to teach her how to tend the vines. How to love and nurture the land. He'd shown her what a real family looked like, how they counted on each other. Sacrificed for one another. How they loved.

But she wasn't one of them.

She shivered and pulled Matt's jacket closer around her. It smelled of him, all spicy and male. Could she really be blamed for shutting her eyes and inhaling his scent? For shoving her arms into the sleeves in an effort to capture the lingering warmth from his body? For wishing, for one spontaneous moment, that instead of his coat being around her, she was in his arms?

God, she never should've had those two glasses—okay, two and a half glasses—of wine. Not only was the alcohol making her maudlin, it was seriously messing up her thoughts. Making her think of things she'd never consider otherwise. Thoughts that only slipped into her mind during her dreams.

The French doors opened and she slouched down so

whoever it was couldn't see her. But when Matt stepped out, his white dress shirt like a beacon in the dark, two plates of food in his hands, she straightened.

"Come on," he said.

Then, without waiting for her to do more than snap her mouth shut, he walked off into the night.

She blinked. Come on? What did that mean? As she watched, he crossed the yard toward the office building.

Well, she wasn't going to just follow him. Now that she had a handle on her emotions, she needed to go inside. Congratulate Brady and J.C. See if Diane could use help with anything. Talk to Aidan. Explain why she was so late.

She stood, held the edges of the coat closed. She sure as hell wasn't going to go with Matt. Not when she felt so raw. So mixed-up. Restless and edgy and…reckless. Enough to do something she was sure to regret.

She took off across the yard toward him, her high heels sinking into the partially frozen ground. When she reached him, her heart raced. From her impromptu jog. No other reason.

He didn't so much as glance her way, just continued to walk, his strides long and purposeful. When they reached the front door, he held out a plate to her. When she just looked at it he said, "Key's in my left pocket. Either you take the plate or you dig for the key."

She practically snatched the plate from him, causing his grin to flash in the darkness.

Her face burned. "Just open the door," she muttered.

Once inside, he shut the door behind her and, with a hand on the small of her back, guided her down the dark hallway. At the door to her office he nudged her inside, handing her the other plate.

"I'll be right there."

Feeling foolish, as if she'd expected something more, she went into her office. Instead of turning on the harsh overhead light, she crossed to her desk, set the plate down and flipped on the lamp. Not wanting anyone at the main house to look across the yard and see a light on, then decide to come over and investigate, she closed the blinds. She was still standing there, staring at the floor, when Matt came in with two bottles of water.

"Here," he said, handing her one. "Eat something. You'll feel better."

Her eyes widened as she took in the amount of food he'd brought her. Shrimp, roast beef, a pasta in cream sauce, asparagus, two different types of rolls and a side salad—heavy on the dressing.

"You must think I have the appetite of a teenage boy," she said as she reluctantly sat down.

He twisted the lid off her water before taking the second bottle with him to the couch. "You do. I've seen you eat, remember?"

Her face heated. Not that she was embarrassed by the amount of food she could consume—a quick metabolism wasn't something to be ashamed of, but embraced. No, what got to her was the idea that he'd noticed her during all those lunches with him and his brothers. The dinners Diane would put on when Matt was home.

He'd noticed her, at least a little bit.

Not wanting to dwell on what that might mean, she shoved the thought aside, pushed the sleeves of his coat up and took a bite of spicy shrimp. He sat on the couch, one arm along the back, as he sipped his water. And watched her.

"The girls still with your ex?" he asked.

She wiped her mouth with the napkin he'd provided. "Until tomorrow. He usually gets them once a month, but since the wedding was adults-only and they were so disappointed about not going, he took them an extra weekend."

Matt's eyebrows shot up. "Big of him."

"He's a good dad. It's just...difficult. What with him being so far away." Difficult for all of them. She'd had to drive two and a half hours to meet him halfway to drop off her daughters.

"And yet you divorced him."

She shrugged. "We wanted different things."

Mainly he wanted to get out of Jewell. And out of their marriage.

"Feeling better?" Matt asked when she set her fork down and tossed her napkin on her plate.

"Yeah." And it was true. Her headache had lessened to a subtle throbbing as opposed to pounding. Her head wasn't as fuzzy. Her stomach settled. "Thanks."

He nodded once, sat up and leaned forward, the bottle of water in his hands between his knees. "So...want to tell me what happened?"

She tore off a piece of roll. Popped it into her mouth

and chewed. God, this was just too surreal. Sitting in her office, just the two of them. She could imagine the sounds of the party. But here, there was almost a hush surrounding them. As if they were the only two people for miles and miles. And now he wanted her to confide in him, to trust him that much?

She couldn't.

He watched her patiently, waiting for her to decide whether or not to answer him. Letting the decision be hers alone. Unlike Aidan, who had no patience when it came to…well…anything. When he asked a question, he demanded an answer. Now. Like his father. Tom had demanded Connie's trust, her loyalty from the first day he'd hired her.

Or maybe she'd given it to him simply because she'd been so pathetically grateful someone was finally giving her a chance. He'd been the father she'd never had after her own had abandoned her and Margaret when being married to a woman with a mental illness became too much for him to bear.

She used to dream her father would come back, that he'd rescue her from her mother and whisk her away somewhere safe where people didn't throw things or cry for hours on end. Where mothers didn't lie in their beds in dark rooms for days at a time. Where she could have clean clothes and hot meals and friends over to play.

Where she would finally be the one taken care of.

Tom may not have done all of those things but he had rescued her in his own way.

Her stomach roiling, she pushed her plate aside. "I

was at my mother's," she said then cleared her throat. "Before I came here."

"She say something to upset you?"

She got to her feet, stared at a shadowy corner of her office. "No, it's not that. It's just..." Facing him, Connie crossed her arms. "She was having one of her episodes. A bad one. It took a while to get her calmed down."

And to clean up the mess. To make sure her mother was bathed and fed. To call Dr. Tweet and see which medications Margaret could safely take that would help her through this.

"That must be hard on you," he said calmly, "having to care for her."

"No...I mean...yeah, it's not easy but she's my mother. What other choice do I have?"

"You could get the state involved."

"Have her committed?" Shaking her head, she took off his coat, tossing it onto a chair as she began to pace. "No. I could never do that."

"Because she's your mother." It wasn't a question.

"Because she's my responsibility."

His eyes on her, he got to his feet. Crossed to her and set both of his warm hands on her shoulders. "See, that's the thing about taking responsibility for another person. Sometimes, it's not always the best thing for you."

God, did he think she didn't know that? There were times, so many times, when all she wanted was to hand over her mother's care to someone else.

But if she did, what kind of person would she be? What kind of daughter?

Besides, she had no idea if the state would get involved. After all, Connie didn't think her mother was a danger to society or even herself, really.

"I can't just abandon her," she said firmly. "I won't. I just…I have to figure out a way to do what's best for her and for myself, that's all."

He slipped one hand to the back of her neck, rubbed the tense muscles. She bit back a groan. "Your mother isn't the only reason you were upset," he said, his voice as soothing as his touch.

She tried to swallow past the sudden lump in her throat. "Believe me, my mother's enough reason for anyone to get upset."

"I'm not doubting that." His fingers slid higher, kneaded the back of her scalp. Her head fell forward slightly to give him better access. "Connie," he asked, his voice husky, his warm breath washing over her face, "what did you mean when you said I was getting everything you ever wanted?"

"I…nothing." She stiffened, tried to pull away, but his hand at her neck didn't loosen. He slid the other hand to the small of her back, dragged her closer to him. Pushing at his chest, she huffed out a breath. "It was the wine."

"No, it wasn't," he murmured, his narrow gaze watching her carefully. "The other night at your house when you said you'd give anything to have what I have…I thought you just said that because you were pissed. That you were just spouting off. Trying to get me to realize what a great opportunity I have, but you weren't. You meant it."

"No, I...I..." To her horror she couldn't meet his eyes. Couldn't force the lie out. So she did what she always did when backed into a corner. Brazened it out. "Look, it's no big—"

"Did Aidan or my mother know you wanted to be a partner in the winery?" he asked, his fingers now combing through her hair, his voice gentle.

She squeezed her eyes shut. Damn him. Why did he have to see in her what no one else had seen?

"No." She thought of the folder in the bottom drawer of her desk. The one with all her hopes and dreams. The one she'd been too afraid to show anyone. Opening her eyes, she glared at Matt. "And if you tell him, I swear to God I will slip into your room while you're sleeping and smother you."

He grinned. "Hey, you can trust me. Anytime I know something Aidan doesn't, I tend to keep it to myself."

"So good to see you haven't outgrown any childish sibling rivalry."

"He started it," Matt said, splaying his fingers at the base of her spine.

Heat speared her. Realizing she still had her hands pressed against his chest, she quickly dropped them. "We should get back."

He stepped forward. She stepped back. Amusement and something hotter shone in his eyes. "Have I told you how amazing you look in that dress?"

Had he? She was having a hard time remembering.

Could barely think with his hand branding her, his fingers in her hair, his touch featherlight, as if she was something precious. Something special. "Uh…I don't think—"

"You're beautiful," he said quietly, causing the words to dry on her tongue. The hand in her hair slid down to the base of her throat, where her pulse beat like a drum. "I can't stop thinking about you. I want to touch you."

Oh, God. She licked her lips. His darkened gaze followed the movement. "No."

"No?"

Not trusting herself to speak, she shook her head.

He tugged her closer. His arousal pressed against her lower belly. He bent his head so that his mouth was mere inches from hers and whispered, "Are you sure?"

Her head swam. Want and need coiled inside of her, tighter and tighter until she feared she'd burst into a million pieces if he stopped now.

Slowly dragging her hands up his arms, she linked them around his neck. And pressed her mouth against his.

CHAPTER TWELVE

HE LIFTED HIS HEAD, searched her eyes for a moment and then, obviously seeing what he needed to see, crashed his mouth down on hers again. The truth was, she wanted him to touch her. When he looked at her with such heat, such hunger, how could she resist?

She slid her hands up to his shoulders, her nails digging into his skin as he backed her roughly against the wall. He pressed the hard length of his body against her, both hands gripping her hips as he kissed her deeper, his tongue sweeping into her mouth.

He placed openmouthed kisses down the length of her throat, across her collarbone. Her head fell back against the wall with a dull thud. His hands moved up her sides to her ribs, his thumbs brushing the sides of her breasts.

"So soft," he murmured huskily. His tongue dipped into the hollow at the base of her throat and she gasped. "You feel so good." He kissed his way up her neck, lightly scraped his teeth over her earlobe before leaning back enough to meet her eyes. "Let me make you feel good, Connie."

She shuddered. The soft demand, the sound of her name in his husky voice, the way he held her, the feel of his arousal against her stomach all combined to be her undoing. She nodded. But instead of kissing her again, he pulled back even farther.

"This is some dress," he said, tracing the tip of his forefinger down one strap. "Think you could wear it again? Like maybe to work Monday?"

She smiled. "I could, but I'd planned on doing more pruning Monday."

"That won't work." He watched his hands as they lightly cupped her breasts. Surely he could feel how her heart pounded? "But maybe you could wear it again sometime," he said. "Just for me."

Her heart stuttered at his words but he didn't mean them to be anything other than flirtatious. They both knew this wasn't the beginning of something. This was a moment. Out of time. Out of reality.

"Maybe," she said, sliding her hands over the breadth of his shoulders, down his arms.

His mouth curved cynically. "Liar," he chided.

Then he brushed his thumbs over her nipples. They peaked. Hardened. Still watching her, he pushed aside the fabric of her bodice, baring one breast, then repeated the movement on the other side. He stared down at her, his eyes glittering, his mouth tense. Her nipples tightened painfully under his hot gaze, her hands clenched his biceps.

Watching her face, he rolled one tight nipple between his thumb and forefinger. Pinched it lightly. A mewling sound rose in her throat. He grinned. And then took her into his mouth. He sucked gently, his tongue rasping across her. She pressed her hips against him, trying to find some release from the ache between her thighs, biting her lower lip to keep from crying out. His free hand worked her other breast until she was panting. She reached down, pressed her palm against his zipper. His arousal twitched against her fingers and she cupped him.

With a low growl he raised his head, kissed her fiercely. She equaled his hunger, her hand stroking him. She could feel his heat through the cloth of his pants. Tugging his shirt free, she skimmed her fingers over his stomach. He inhaled sharply then hissed out a breath. But when she attempted to unfasten his belt, he jerked back and spun her around in one smooth move. She slapped her palms against the wall to catch her balance, her breath whooshing out of her lungs.

She tried to turn but he held her hips immobile in his big, strong hands. "Matt, I—"

"Shh…" The low rumble of his voice scraped over her like a touch. He kissed the nape of her neck. "Trust me."

She swallowed and willed her tense muscles to relax. With a grunt that could've been satisfaction, he tugged on her hips, forcing her to take a step back from the wall. Dragging the tight skirt of her dress up her legs slowly, his hands left a heated path along the backs of her knees. Her thighs. He bunched the material at her waist then smoothed his hands over her hips, across her stomach. His fingers dipped under the elastic edge of her panties. Stilled. She sucked in a breath, pushed her hips back, but his hand went no further.

"Matt," she gasped as he sucked gently on her neck. "Please."

As if that's what he was waiting for, he shoved her panties down and touched her, his hand rough against her, his fingers seeking. He slid one finger inside her, then slowly out again, and she whimpered. Pressed her hips forward. He stroked her, his touch sure, his other hand reaching around to cup her breast. He placed biting kisses along her neck and back. She whimpered. Her blood heated. Raced through her veins as the sensations built. Peaked. Her hands scraped against the wall, looking for something solid to hold on to, something to keep her grounded when she felt as if she was splintering apart.

"It's okay," Matt said into her ear, his arm tight around her waist. "Let go. I've got you."

She came with a hoarse cry, her head thrown back against his shoulder, her hips pumping against his hand. Pleasure coursed through her, washed over her until she was gasping, her limbs heavy. Her knees weak.

Gulping in air, she stared blindly at the ceiling. Matt's shoulder was solid beneath her head, his lips warm as he pressed a kiss to her temple. His arousal hard at her back. But as her body cooled and her pulse slowed, reality began to set in.

She'd used him. She'd used Matt to help her forget. To make her feel special. Wanted. She'd been completely selfish.

Just like her mother.

MATT DIDN'T LOOSEN HIS hold on her. Not yct. He pressed a kiss behind her ear and breathed in her sweet scent.

"Spend the night with me," he said.

She went absolutely still and he winced. Damn it. Wrong thing to say. He should've kept his mouth shut. He sure as hell hadn't meant to sound quite so desperate. But he was hard and aching for her. And after the way she'd just come apart in his arms... He blew out a heavy breath. What else was he supposed to do? Just let her go?

"I can't," she said.

"Can't? Or won't?"

"Does it matter?"

"Yeah. It docs," he said gruffly, surprised to find he meant it. If any other woman had rcjcctcd him, he'd have accepted it as gracefully as possible and moved on. Then again, he couldn't remember wanting a woman the way he wanted Connie.

But she just shook her head, her soft, sweet-smelling hair tickling his nose. "Please let go of me," she said, her voice cracking.

He immediately dropped his arms and stepped back. As soon as he did, she yanked up her panties and tugged down her skirt, wiggling her hips to smooth the fabric in place.

He gritted his teeth together. "Want to talk about it?"

She glanced over her shoulder as she adjusted the top of her dress. "No."

Stubborn to the very end. Why the hell had he ever found that appealing? Shoving a hand through his hair, he paced to the door and back again, his body hard and aching. He needed to backtrack, to get this situation under control. His control.

"Why don't we sit down?" he asked, keeping his tone calm. He had a feeling she was at the breaking point and the last thing he wanted was to push her. "We can discuss—"

"There's nothing to discuss," she said, facing him, her cheeks still flushed from her orgasm, her lipstick smudged from his kisses. "I just…don't want to sleep with you."

Anger, denial, lust, all surged, pushed him to stalk toward her. Her eyes widened and for each step he took, she took one back until she bumped into the wall. But he still edged closer until there were only a few inches between them. A mistake, he knew. What he needed most right now was distance, but he couldn't stop himself. Just as he couldn't stop from dragging his finger along her jaw, then over her lower lip. He kept his finger pressed gently there, against the softness of her mouth.

"You sure about that?" he asked quietly.

She shivered. Her eyes darkened. Her lips parted.

And then she bit him.

"Ow!" He snatched his finger back. Rubbed his thumb over the stinging flesh. "Son of a bitch."

Looking supremely satisfied with herself, she crossed her arms. "Serves you right."

He blinked. Then barked out a short laugh. "You're right." She really pushed his buttons. And made him want to push her back. To get her to admit she felt the same awareness, the same incessant pull for him that he felt for her. Holding his hands up in an I-surrender gesture, he stepped back. "I did deserve that." And possibly worse. "You have every right to say no. I guess I was just hoping to change your mind."

"Don't do that," she snapped.

He frowned. "Don't do what?"

"Don't be all charming and…and understanding and…nice."

"Okay," he said slowly. "Let me get this straight. You want me to be an ass?"

She looked at him as if he was the one spouting crazy talk. "You just want me because I'm convenient," she blurted.

Brady's voice filled Matt's head. *There's nothing easy about Connie. And you're all about easy.*

Disappointment and anger coiled inside of him. That he'd thought she'd seen through to the real him.

"First of all," he managed in what he considered a highly reasonable tone, "a microwave is convenient. Having your keys on the hook by the damn door on your way out is convenient. But believe me, you—and this damn hunger I have for you—are most definitely not convenient."

Her mouth worked soundlessly for a few seconds then she cleared her throat. "Look, just because we're attracted to each other doesn't mean we have to act on it."

His blood heated. "If you're trying to get me to back off," he said hoarsely, "admitting you're attracted to me is the wrong way to go about it."

She blushed. "There's just too much between us for this to go any further."

"Seems to me there's too much between us for this not to go any further."

"I'm not talking about sparks. I mean…we have a history. Plus, you're my boss." She ticked each item off on her fingers. "Or at least you will be. And think about how weird it would be for your family." Her eyes widened. "Think of Diane."

Tucking his shirt back into his pants, he laughed shortly. "I hate to break it to you, but when I'm with a beautiful woman, a woman I'm sexually attracted to, the last person I think about is my mother."

She swallowed. "Yeah, well, I'm thinking of her. I'm thinking how completely awkward it would be if we had sex and she found out. No. It can't happen. It'd change everything. This whole—" she gestured wildly between them "—thing was a mistake." Lifting her chin, she straightened. "We both need to forget it ever happened."

He watched her walk to the door, her hips swaying

in that damn dress, the slight roundness of her shoulders suggesting a vulnerability he'd never expected, or particularly cared to see in her.

He waited until she'd opened the door before he spoke. "What if I don't want to forget it?" he asked, watching her carefully.

But she didn't look back. "We don't always get what we want," she said, her tone so sad, so resigned, he clasped his hands behind his back so he wouldn't reach for her. "Not even you."

LATE FRIDAY AFTERNOON, Connie stood at the top of the stairs in Diane's house. She inhaled deeply and held her breath for the count of five. Okay. She could do this. It was only Aidan after all. There wasn't anything to be scared of. Certainly nothing that warranted the trembling of her hands or the butterflies doing somersaults in her stomach.

She had a plan. A good one. Her fingers tightened on the folder she carried. She'd spent the entire week thinking about how to approach Aidan with the idea. Now all she had to do was suck it up and do it already.

Ever since she'd tipsily let it slip that she thought the Diamond Dust should host weddings, she hadn't been able to stop thinking about it. And the more she thought, the more she realized what a great idea it was. Hosting special events could really boost the winery's bottom line.

Plus, if Aidan and Diane went for it, it would help cement her place at the winery. Ensure that even if Matt pushed her out of the vineyards, she'd still be a part of the Diamond Dust.

And while Matt had thought it was a bad idea—and she'd even said Aidan would agree with him—she wanted to present her case anyway. After all, Aidan was a reasonable man.

Reasonable. Stubborn. A bit arrogant.

She sighed. This was such a bad idea.

But she was going through with it anyway. She had to. She wanted to prove she was more than just the vineyard manager. That she had a stake in what happened at the winery. Damn it, she wanted to be included.

Besides, while she may not be a part of the Sheppard family, she was a part of the Diamond Dust. A valued part. Which meant her ideas would have to be taken seriously.

Before she could talk herself out of it, she knocked on Aidan's office door. A moment later he called, "Come in."

She opened the door and stepped inside. "Do you have a—oh." She froze to see all three Sheppard brothers staring at her. Her hand squeezed the door handle. "Sorry. I didn't realize you were busy."

Just as she was about to back out into the hallway, Aidan waved her in from behind his desk. "We were done."

"Right," Matt said in his low, lazy voice as he slouched on the sofa, his head resting on the back. "Doesn't take long for the president over here to shoot down any and all ideas."

"Give me some good ideas," Aidan said mildly, "and I wouldn't have to shoot them down."

"They've been like this for the past hour," Brady said from his seat across from Aidan's desk. "Save me."

"I'd hate to interrupt," she said quickly, already taking a step back. "I can—"

"Please, interrupt," Brady said. "I'm begging you."

Not seeing any other choice, and not wanting to be a coward like she'd been with her partnership proposal, she forced her feet to move forward. As she crossed the room, she felt Matt's gaze on her.

Crap. Why did he have to be here? She'd done an admirable job of avoiding him for almost an entire week. Not an easy task given they'd both been in the vineyards pruning every day. But she'd managed. If he walked into a room, she made an excuse to walk out. If he was pruning the Petit Verdot grapes, she worked on the Merlot. She'd hoped to keep her distance from him for the next…oh…twelve months or so. Because each time she saw him, she alternated between congratulating herself and kicking her own ass for not taking him home the other night.

And now she had to pitch her idea in front of him. An idea she already knew he wasn't gung ho about.

Connie perched on the edge of the chair next to Brady. Then again, maybe he'd been right when he told her Aidan would agree with an idea if he knew Matt was against it.

What did she have to lose?

"Where are the girls?" Matt asked, glancing at his watch. "Shouldn't they be done with school by now?

She bit the inside of her cheek. Did he have to talk to her? It would be so much easier to pretend he didn't exist if he didn't actually speak. Especially directly to her. Even better if he didn't act as if he was concerned about her daughters. The same kids who obviously scared him to death. "I already picked them up," she said, staring down at her folder as if searching for a paper so she could avoid his eyes. "They're out in the yard playing with Lily."

"What's up?" Aidan asked.

Setting the folder on the edge of his desk, she swallowed. "Ever since Brady and J.C.'s wedding, I've been thinking about how great it would be for the Diamond Dust to host special events."

Aidan sat back, steepled his fingers at his chest. "We don't have the facilities—"

"We do," she insisted, leaning forward. "Or we could if we converted the barn—or even the carriage house—into a reception hall."

"There's plenty of empty land, too," Brady pointed out. When everyone stared at him in surprise, he lifted a shoulder. "It's actually something I've thought about before. Most other wineries do it."

"We're not other wineries," Aidan said dismissively. "Our focus is to be a single estate winery making superior wine. Not to throw parties for other people so they can get their picture taken in front of a vineyard. And not," he added, looking at Matt, "to make a generic product so that one of us can get pats on his back."

"Here we go," Brady murmured, pinching the bridge of his nose.

Matt slowly unfolded from the couch, his heated gaze belying his easy movement. "There's nothing generic about my wines."

"All the wines you make, whether in California, France or Australia, are similar. Your technique doesn't vary based on where you are, so you can make some homogenous product that wins medals." Aidan twirled a pen in his fingers. "Our goal is to make wine with individual character based on our terroir and Virginia's history of winemaking."

Matt laughed harshly. "You sound just like Dad."

Aidan narrowed his eyes. "I'll take that as a compliment."

"You would," Matt said with a shake of his head.

Connie's heart thumped heavily to see them facing off. To see the hurt and anger in Matt's eyes. And she hated that Matt was too stubborn, or too busy trying to prove himself, to see that in this case, Aidan was right.

But maybe, just maybe, Matt was right, too.

And that thought would get her nothing but trouble. The last thing she needed was to go against Aidan. He was her boss. Her friend. The man she'd known and worked with for the past eight years.

He was the one she needed on her side. And she didn't

want Matt, or her confused feelings about him, messing up her life.

"You two can fight later," she said, wanting to defuse the situation. "Let's get back to discussing my idea now."

"There's nothing to discuss," Aidan said, and though she could've sworn she heard an apology in his voice, it didn't soften the blow any. "We'd need a hell of a lot of capital to convert the barn or carriage house into the type of facility you're suggesting. Capital I'm not sure we'd recoup by having someone's grandparents' fiftieth anniversary party here. Not to mention, that sort of sideline would take time away from other aspects of the business."

Meaning he wasn't even willing to hear her out. Her eyes stung but she'd be damned if she'd let one single tear fall in front of him. In front of any of them. "I...it was just an idea."

Her idea. One she wanted to see become a reality.

"You're forgetting something," Matt said. Connie glanced at him but he wasn't looking at her. He was talking to Aidan. "This isn't your decision to make. At least, not solely your decision." He nodded at Brady. "All three of us get a say."

"The partnership papers haven't been drawn up yet," Aidan said stiffly.

"Doesn't mean we can't vote on whether or not to at least consider Connie's idea," Matt said easily. "Or, she could take this directly to Mom. Seeing as how she's still sole owner."

Connie blinked. Was he supporting her? A small kernel of hope lodged itself in her chest but she ruthlessly tamped it down. No need to get excited yet. Just because Matt was willing to hear her out didn't mean he'd rethought the issue and was on her side.

Aidan stood, his curious gaze flicking between her and Matt. "You want to vote? Fine. You know what I think."

"That's not necessary," Connie said, standing as well, leaving Brady the only one still seated. How could he sit there while his brothers looked as if they wanted to rip into each other? And though she appreciated Matt trying to help her out, she had enough drama in dealing with her mother. The Diamond Dust was supposed to be her safe zone. A place for her to escape all of that. "It's not like I have all that much invested in the idea," she said, hoping to end this thing here and now.

All three men ignored her. And didn't that bode well for her future place at the winery?

"Can't hurt to discuss it," Brady said. "Keep our options open."

"I agree with Brady," Matt said smoothly. Connie's mouth dropped. The previously squashed hope soared. "It's decided."

And then she saw it. Matt's cocky stance—head tilted, thumbs hooked into his pockets. The triumph in his eyes as he smirked at his brother.

Damn him.

"The hell it is." Hands fisted at her sides, she stepped over Brady's outstretched legs and marched across the room to Matt. She poked him in the chest. "What kind of game are you playing?"

Frowning, he rubbed where her finger had drilled into him. "It's no game. We had a vote and—"

"And nothing." It took all of her willpower not to smack him upside his too-handsome head. "You don't want to hold special events here. You told me that at the wedding."

"You two have already discussed this?" Aidan asked, coming out from behind his desk. "Why is this the first I've heard of it?"

"Shut up, Aidan," Matt said tightly, not taking his eyes off her. "Believe it or not, some people hold conversations that don't involve you."

Angry, and so humiliated she could barely see straight, Connie shook her head. "Why are you doing this?"

Matt's mouth tightened. Taking hold of her elbow, he pulled her aside and bent his head to say into her ear, "I'm trying to help you."

She met his eyes. He seemed sincere. But this was Matt Sheppard she was dealing with. He was an expert actor. So very accomplished at playing whatever part he thought would get him what he wanted.

She jerked away from him. "No. You're doing this for yourself." Her voice shook with anger. And hurt. "I want you to listen to me and listen good, boyo," she said, ignoring the way his gaze went flat and his expression darkened at the use of his dad's old nickname for him. "Don't you ever…ever…use me as some sort of way to screw with your brother or to prove yourself to your family. You want to spend your life fighting with your family, playing the part of the poor, misunderstood outcast, that's fine. But don't you dare drag me into the middle of your insecurities."

Then, without so much as glancing at the other men in the room, she turned on her heel and stormed out of the room in all her righteous fury.

CHAPTER THIRTEEN

"WHAT WAS THAT?" AIDAN asked after Connie made an exit worthy of any drama queen. He hadn't known she'd had it in her. The way she'd laid into Matt? That had been inspired. And, it seemed, heartfelt.

If he wasn't so irritated, he'd be mighty impressed.

He crossed to Matt. "What the hell was that?" he repeated.

"Nothing." Matt's gaze was still on the door as if he were willing Connie to return.

"It didn't look like nothing. What did you do to her?"

Matt bristled. Took a step closer, his shoulders rigid, his eyes narrowed to slits. "Stay out of it," he said softly. Dangerously.

Aidan rolled his shoulders back. Though Matt had a good two inches and twenty pounds on him, for just one moment, he seriously wished his brother would take a swing at him. It wouldn't solve anything, but at the moment, he didn't care.

"That's enough," Brady said, pushing his way between them. He had on his ex-Marine face, all hard eyes and take-no-shit expression. "Matt, go outside and cool off." When Matt didn't move, Brady raised an eyebrow. "Now."

His deadly tone must've gotten through Matt's thick head because he sneered then walked away.

Aidan exhaled heavily. "I don't like how he looks at her."

"What?"

He crossed to the window. "Matt. I don't like how he looks at Connie."

"Not your business."

Aidan glanced out the window to see Payton and Abby under a tree, petting Lily. "Connie is my business."

"She's a grown woman," Brady pointed out as he retook his seat. He picked up the folder Connie had left behind. "And as she just proved, she's more than capable of handling anything Matt dishes out."

As Aidan watched, Connie made it halfway across the yard, then stopped and pulled her phone out of her pocket.

Aidan crossed his arms and leaned back against the windowsill. "She's like a sister."

"I'm guessing Matt doesn't think of her as a sister," Brady murmured with one of his rare grins.

"What's that supposed to mean?" He straightened. "You know something."

He didn't look up from the papers he was reading. "I know many things. Including when to keep my mouth shut."

That was the understatement of the decade.

"I just don't want her to get hurt," Aidan said.

"That's not up to you."

No, but it should be. And he couldn't just stand by and watch Matt play games with Connie. She deserved better than that. And he didn't deserve the headaches he'd get dealing with the two of them being at each other's throats all the time. Matt had been involved in the Diamond Dust for only a few weeks and already he'd disrupted how things worked around here.

"You should look at these," Brady said, flipping through papers. "She's really done her homework about this special events venue."

"I don't need to look at them. We're not doing it."

Brady gave him a hooded stare then tossed the folder on the desk as he stood. "If you'd take that stick out of your ass, you might realize we're not the enemy here. You don't have to control everything. We all want what's best for the Diamond Dust. Even Matt."

And with that, Brady walked away.

Damn it, he knew that. And he wasn't trying to control everything.

Things just worked better, went more smoothly when he was in charge.

"PAYTON ELIZABETH HENKEL," Connie said through her teeth later that evening, "I'm not going to tell you again. Put your coat on."

She opened the front door and about had a heart attack to find Matt standing on her porch, a glower on his face, his crossed arms pulling his jacket tight across his broad shoulders.

Once her heartbeat resumed beating somewhat normally, she frowned. "It's really not a good time," she said, pitching her voice so he could hear her over Abby's loud wailing. God, you'd think the kid was being tortured the way she was carrying on.

"Why'd you do it?" he asked.

She frowned. "I've done so many things. You're going to have to be more specific."

"Why'd you suggest the winery start hosting events? The real reason—not what you told my brothers."

"I told your brothers the truth."

He shook his hair back. "Part of it. I want to know the rest."

Abby's wail went up an octave. Connie winced. "Look, I don't have time for this—"

"Then you'd better say it quick, because I'm not moving from this spot until you do."

And wouldn't that be the perfect addition to what was rapidly becoming a crappy evening. "I just...I thought it would be something that could help the winery grow."

He studied her so intently, she had to force herself not to squirm. "Who did you plan on having organize this new venture? Who would be in charge of it?"

Picking up her coat so she could avoid meeting his eyes, she shrugged. "I thought I would."

"Because you don't want to work in the vineyards anymore. Because you don't want to work with me."

It wasn't the flatness of his tone that had her head snapping up, but the hurt underneath it. "No. It's not... it's not personal. But I have to face facts. There's no reason for both of us to run the vineyard. So I thought if we hosted events, I'd still have a place at the winery." She bit her lower lip. "That I'd still be needed there."

And admitting that was one of the hardest things she'd ever done.

"You'll always have a place at the Diamond Dust," he said gruffly. "And you were right when you said I was just trying to provoke Aidan by agreeing with your idea. I apologize."

What did it matter? Her position at the winery was still in jeopardy—everything she'd ever wanted was still out of her reach. And she really didn't need Matt at her door, questioning her motives, throwing her for a loop with his apology and hooded gaze. Especially not now. Besides, it was easier for her peace of mind when she was mad at him.

"Apology accepted," she said jabbing her arm into the sleeve of her coat. "Thanks for stopping by. Girls," she called, turning her back on him and hoping like mad no one noticed the slight edge of hysteria in her tone, "let's go."

Abby walked across the living room, head down, feet dragging as if she was walking the last mile. "I don't want to go to Grandma's." She sniffed loudly as fresh tears fell. "It smells funny."

Connie handed her a crumpled tissue from her coat pocket. "Hold your nose. Payton," she snapped, seeing her older daughter still sitting on the couch, arms crossed, a mulish expression her face. "Come on."

"No."

Connie froze. "Excuse me?"

"I said no."

Yeah. That's what Connie had thought she'd said. "I don't have time for this. Get. In. The. Car."

Payton shook her head so hard, her ponytail hit her cheeks. "No. I'm not going to Grandma's. Abby's right. It smells funny. And Grandma's mean."

True. If the girls didn't give her enough attention or, heaven forbid, took Connie's from her Margaret acted like a spoiled child. Which was why Connie rarely took the girls to visit and she never left them there alone. God only knew what Margaret would say to them. But this was an emergency—or at least, according to her mother it was—so the girls had to go with her.

Connie crossed to the couch and stood over her daughter, her hands fisted on her hips. "Either you get your butt in that car right now," she said in what she considered a highly reasonable tone, "or I swear—"

"Everything okay here?"

Biting back a scream, Connie closed her eyes at the sound of Matt's calm voice. "Just dandy. Can't you tell?"

"Anything I can do to help?"

She opened her mouth to say no. To tell him she'd handle this, that she'd take care of it as she always did. On her own. But she glanced at her daughters. Abby had silent tears streaking down her cheeks while Payton glared, her mouth set in a thin line. Guilt over trying to force her daughters to do something they so obviously didn't want to do curdled her stomach.

And Matt stood just inside her door, all big and solid and sexy in his expensive coat and windblown hair, witnessing her spiral out of control.

God, she was just so tired. So very tired of doing everything on her own. What would it hurt, just this once, to ask for help?

"Can I speak to you for a moment?" She dragged him back outside before he could answer—and before she could change her mind. She shut the door and leaned back against it. "I need your help," she said in a rush.

"What's going on?"

"It's my mom. She…she just called. Well, actually, she's been calling for the past six hours but she's been getting more frantic." She swallowed. "I have to go over there but Abby's crying and Payton's furious…well, you already saw that, didn't you? I really don't want to take them with me because I never know what to expect when I get there. What sort of condition my mom's going to be in, and I was just wondering if maybe you could… watch my kids?"

He was silent for a few moments, then he shook his head. Cleared his throat. "What?"

Her stomach sank. "Never mind. You probably already have plans." After all, it was a Friday night. And she couldn't imagine Matt spending it alone. "It's just that your mom's in D.C. with Al, and if I asked anyone else I'd have to explain the whole situation and…" She stopped long enough to take a breath. "It was a dumb idea anyway."

A dumb, desperate idea. She should know better

than to try to take the easy way out, she thought as she opened the door.

"I don't have any plans."

She whirled around. "You don't?"

He shrugged. "I can stay with them."

"You're sure?" Now that she had time to think about it, maybe this wasn't the best idea. After all, the last time she'd left him alone with her daughters, it'd taken only ten minutes before he'd bailed. "Because, you know, I probably won't be very long. And they need to learn they can't get their way because they cry or throw a tantrum."

"They do need to learn that. But I'd say in this case you could probably make an exception."

He was right. When it came to her mother, she found herself making lots of exceptions. But if leaving Matt in charge of her daughters meant saving them from witnessing Margaret's mania, well…what choice did she have?

"Okay. That's…great. Thank you so much." Opening the door, she grabbed her purse and car keys off the side table. "Girls, Matt's going to stay here while I run to Grandma's."

"We don't have to go?" Abby asked, her cheeks stained with dried tear marks.

"Not this time." She pulled some cash out of her wallet. "But that doesn't mean I'm happy with how you both behaved. And we will be discussing it when I get home."

Their faces fell.

"I should be back in half an hour," Connie told Matt as she held out the money to him. "An hour at the most."

He just looked at it. "I hadn't realized I was getting paid. Will I have to claim this on my taxes?"

"Ha, ha. It's not payment—it's so you can order some dinner. We haven't had time to eat yet."

He took off his jacket and held it, obviously having no desire to take her money. "I figured I'd just give them a few dry bread crusts and water." The girls looked at him—Abby in horror, Payton in infatuation. As if she'd gobble up anything he fed her.

Oh, this was such a bad idea.

But she was doing it. Her phone vibrated in her pocket. She didn't need to look at it to know it was her mother demanding to know when Connie would get there.

She rubbed her temple, tried to stave off the headache brewing there. "Okay. I'll just leave the money—" she laid it on the end table next to a photo of Abby and Payton from last year's dance recital "—and you can figure out dinner." She kissed both girls on the top of their heads. "Love you. Be good."

Matt walked with her to the door.

"I really appreciate this," she told him. "Oh, you have my cell number, right? In case you need anything?"

"If not, I have the number for 9-1-1 memorized." She must've looked stricken, because he smiled. "I was kidding. Relax. We'll be fine."

She sighed. "No. I know you will be. Sorry, I'm just a little…"

"Paranoid?"

"Cautious," she said, trying to hide a shudder. Margaret suffered from paranoia. But that wasn't Connie. She was nothing like her mother. Besides, she trusted Matt. And to prove it she lifted her hand in a wave and walked away.

"KEN'S BEEN WORKING OUT," Matt said of the six-pack abs the plastic doll was sporting.

He sat on Connie's living room floor with Abby. Since Connie had left two hours ago, they'd played "Dance Dance Revolution" while waiting for the pizza he'd ordered to be delivered. They'd eaten, played a hand of Uno, two rounds of Operation and had even attempted Trivial Pursuit, the Disney edition, until the girls felt so sorry for him getting every question wrong, Abby suggested they play with her Barbie dolls.

Barbie. What the hell had happened to him? Luckily, his initial panic over being responsible for two little girls had waned and he was now just comfortably out of his element. A good thing, since Connie had called more than thirty minutes ago and said she'd be later than she'd originally thought.

"And what's with the tattoo?" he asked, frowning at Ken and the tribal tat on his right biceps.

"That's not Ken," Abby said, tugging a skirt around Barbie. "That's Jacob."

While she hadn't completely lost her shyness around

him, at least she was speaking to him. Which he considered a great triumph. For the first hour, anything she wanted him to know she told Payton, who in turn would speak for her sister.

"Who's Jacob?" he asked. "The younger brother?"

"He's a werewolf," Payton said from the couch where she was writing something with colored pencil. "From *Twilight*."

Matt frowned. "A werewolf, huh? Is that why he doesn't have a shirt?"

Abby shrugged, while Payton said, "Yes. He's too hot to wear a shirt."

"Hot as in…too warm?" He sincerely hoped that's what she meant.

Unfortunately, she shook her head. "No, Jacob's hot. You know—" she widened her eyes "hot. Like Zac Efron."

Matt had no idea who Zac Efron was, but he got her gist. "Are you sure you're only eight?" Wasn't that too young to be thinking guys were hot?

"Eight and almost a half," she said primly.

He grinned. "How could I forget that almost half?"

Abby hopped her Barbie across the floor to him. "I'm going to the grocery store," she said in a falsetto. It took Matt a moment to realize she wasn't talking to him, she was being the doll talking to Ken. Er…Jacob.

"Hey, can you drop me off at the gym?" he asked, deepening his voice. "Werewolves don't get abs like these sitting around eating cupcakes, you know."

"Sure," Abby said. Then, humming, she put Jacob and

Barbie in a pink plastic convertible and pushed the car across the living room, dropping Jacob off in a corner before continuing over to the spot where they'd set up a grocery store complete with shopping cart, cash register and tiny plastic food.

Matt rolled onto his back, then reached beneath him and pulled out a toy dog that was digging into his spine. Linking his hands behind his head, he looked over at Payton. "What are you doing? Getting a head start on your homework?"

She slid the blue pencil back into the box and took out a red one. "It's a card for Mom."

"Ahh…trying to get on her good side, huh?"

Her lips twitched, reminding him so much of Connie he had to stop himself from laughing out loud. "It's saying I'm sorry," she told him, her brow furrowed as she concentrated. Finally she lifted her head. "Do you think it's okay to say you're sorry even if you don't really mean it?"

"You're asking the wrong guy. I never apologize unless I mean it."

As he'd done with Connie earlier. As much as he'd wanted to place the blame directly on her, to pretend she'd just overreacted, he couldn't. Not when she'd been right. He had been trying to piss off Aidan. He'd just gone about it the wrong way.

"Well, I really am sorry for being mean to Mom," Payton said quickly. "I'm just not sorry that I didn't have to go to Grandma's house."

"It smells funny there," Abby piped up, then went back to playing with her dolls.

He jackknifed into a sitting position. "I'm guessing your mom understands your reasons for not wanting to go there." Otherwise she never would've asked him to babysit.

Especially after she'd ignored him for almost an entire week.

A week where he'd been trying to get her out of his mind after their...encounter at the wedding.

"My mom said I can't invite you to my dance recital," Payton said, watching him intently. "She said you probably won't be able to come."

"She said that, huh?" But had she said it as a way to gently let her daughter down? Or because she didn't want him to attend?

Probably a bit of the former and a whole hell of a lot of the latter.

And why that ticked him off to no end, Matt had no idea.

"Will you?" she asked.

"Will I what?"

She gave an eye roll worthy of any teenager. The kid sure was advanced. "Will you be able to come?"

His stomach twisted. How was he supposed to answer that? He could say no, but he hated lying to the kid when there was no reason he couldn't go.

Females. Always wanting a commitment.

"Actually, I'm not sure what I'll be doing in May," he hedged.

"That's okay," she said with a sigh. "My dad can't come, either. He doesn't live here anymore and he said it was too far to drive just to watch me for ten minutes."

Matt flinched. She was killing him. But no matter how much he wanted to tell her that he'd be there, he wouldn't. He didn't make promises. They were too easy to break.

"Why don't you finish that card and come down here with us?" he asked instead of telling her what he really wanted to say. *Don't put your faith in me. Don't expect too much from me.*

The way she looked at him, as if she knew damn well what he was trying to do, unnerved him. "I'll be done in a minute," she finally said, her voice sad, as if she'd made the mistake of believing he was different. That he wouldn't let her down.

Damn it, that wasn't his fault. He approached his life one day at a time, living in the moment instead of worrying about what might happen tomorrow. He didn't want her to count on him. It was too much responsibility. Too much pressure.

Too damn frightening having someone put their trust in him that way.

Too much of a chance to prove his family had been right about him all along.

CHAPTER FOURTEEN

CONNIE PRESSED THE PALMS of her hands against her eyes and inhaled deeply. Then frowned. Abby was right. Her mother's house did smell funny. Kneeling on the floor in front of the bedroom closet, she leaned back on her heels and lifted the lid off yet another shoe box. Stacks of them covered the closet floor. They were various sizes and filled with everything from old photos and take-out menus to screws, dead batteries and, in one memorable find, a can of soup with an expiration date of two years ago.

Margaret had everything in those boxes, it seemed, except for the gold, heart-shaped locket she'd picked up at a garage sale a few years ago. The tarnished, heart-shaped locket that she probably had never worn.

The necklace Connie had been trying to help her mother find for the past two hours.

"Mom," she said, "I think we're just going to have to accept that we're not going to find it."

"Oh, we have to find it," Margaret cried as she tossed aside the lid to another box, her movements jerky, her words coming fast and furious. "It's my favorite necklace."

Connie bit her lower lip. Right. And she'd wanted it

so badly, she'd called Connie half a dozen times, demanding she come over and help her look for it. By the time Connie got there, Margaret had taken every item out of both dressers and had gone through at least ten shoe boxes, scattering the items across the bed.

Oh, Connie didn't doubt the necklace was in the house. Somewhere. After all, Margaret collected things. She didn't throw them out.

Connie put the contents back in the shoe box and set the lid on top. "Well, I give up. I don't know where it could be."

Okay, that was a lie. She knew damn well it could be in one of the twenty or so boxes still left in the closet. Or maybe a kitchen drawer. But she'd been looking for an ugly, cheap necklace way too long already. And she was done.

"You don't want me to find it," Margaret said, accusingly. Her red sweatpants and matching sweatshirt swallowed her thin frame. Her eyes widened then narrowed. "You hid it!"

Used to her mother's mood swings—and unfounded accusations—Connie wearily got to her feet. "Why on earth would I hide your necklace?"

"How would I know what goes through your mind, Constance? You probably hid it just to spite me."

"Mom, listen to me," Connie said, speaking as if to a three-year-old in the midst of a tantrum. "I did not hide your necklace."

"Then you took it," she said, her tone horrified. "Or else that horrible nurse who was here last week stole it.

That's it, isn't it? She stole it and you're protecting her, but it won't work. I want my necklace back."

And though she knew it was futile to argue with her mother, that it only seemed to feed Margaret's delusions, Connie couldn't stop herself. "Mom, that nurse was sent here to help you. I'm sure she didn't take your necklace."

"She did. I know she did. I'm calling the police!" Margaret snatched up the cordless phone so quickly, the base fell to the floor with a crash. "She won't get away with this. She should be thrown in jail!"

Connie stabbed her hands through her hair and then just held on to her head, hoping the pressure was enough to stop her brain from exploding.

Her hands shaking, Margaret pressed a button. It must've been the wrong one because she swore, clicked the phone off then tried again.

"Wait," Connie said, reaching for it, but Margaret skipped backward. "There's no need to call the police. I'm sure the necklace is here. I'll keep looking for it, okay?"

But when she met her mother's eyes and saw the satisfaction there, Connie's breath caught. She'd done it again. Given in to her mother to keep the peace. In a pitiful attempt to make her mother happy. To make her healthy.

Except she wasn't healthy. And no matter how many times she gave in, no matter how often she gave her mother what she wanted, Connie would never be able to make her happy.

A sense of despair washed over her. Dear God, she was never going to be free of this vicious cycle.

See, that's the thing about taking responsibility for another person. Sometimes, it's not always the best thing for you.

Her head spun as the realization hit her with the force of a backhanded slap. Matt was right. Acquiescing to her mother's illness, her demands, wasn't what was best for her. It never had been. And it never would be.

Worse than that? It wasn't good for her mother, either. Margaret needed help, more help than Connie could give her. And by trying to take care of Margaret on her own, she'd ignored the reality that her mother's mental health had declined over the past few years.

Connie shook her head sadly and took her mother's soft hands in hers. "You're not well," she said as gently as possible. This was, after all, her mother. "You need help."

Margaret's eyes filled and she tugged free of Connie's hold. "You're trying to get rid of me. You want to…to… send me to some horrible home."

"If you'd take your medicine—"

"I can't," she wailed as loudly and with as much heartfelt emotion as Abby had done earlier that night. "Those pills make me sick to my stomach. I told you that! And Dr. Tweet agrees with me."

"No," Connie said wearily, "he doesn't."

As usual, her mother believed only what she wanted to believe. And when she saw a doctor, she heard only whatever helped her keep her delusions.

"Will you start listening to me and Dr. Tweet?" Connie asked, her nerves taut, her throat so tight she had to force the words out. "Will you start taking the medicine the doctor prescribed, regularly?"

"I don't need it."

"If you don't take your pills…" Connie had to stop, clear her throat. "If you don't take them, if you don't allow a nurse to come over here several times a week to check on you, then I'm going to have to look into finding you somewhere else to live. Somewhere safe."

Margaret's eyes were huge, her mouth wobbled. "I won't go," she said, her voice thick. "I won't leave my home. How could you do this to me, Constance? How could you treat me this way after all I've done for you? What kind of daughter are you?"

"The kind who's given up her life for you," she said quietly, "who lets you manipulate me into dropping everything to do as you ask. I'm sorry, but I can't do that, can't be that person any longer. You need to be somewhere safe, where there's trained staff to take care of you. And I need to put myself and my daughters first."

Connie walked out of the house and didn't take a full breath until she was behind the wheel of her car. Trembling, eyes stinging with unshed tears, she rolled down her window and gulped in the cold night air until her heart rate steadied. Until she had regained enough control to pull away from the curb. Then she drove away from the house she'd grown up in. From the woman who'd given birth to her. Who'd raised her in a world of neglect and delusions and selfishness.

She didn't look back.

MATT WOKE WITH A START, snorting as he raised his head from the back of the couch. Eyes squinted, mind fuzzy with sleep, he watched Connie step inside the living room. He tried not to move, since Abby had her head resting against his left side, her neck stretched at an odd angle, her mouth open in sleep. Payton was curled up at his right. With a soft moan, she stretched, her bare heels digging into his ribs before she snuggled down into the couch cushion, her hands folded under her cheek.

Being careful not to disturb the girls, he slowly sat up. Rubbed both hands over his face and blew out a breath. He frowned when he noticed Connie hadn't moved from just inside the doorway. Her eyes were wide as she stared at the sight of various toys, games and Barbie accessories strewn across her living-room floor. She trembled, her keys clinking softly in her hand, the light from the TV illuminating her pale face. The starkness in her eyes.

What the hell?

"Hey," he whispered, shifting Abby to the side so he could stand. "You okay?"

But she just shook her head and, stepping over the mess, walked into the kitchen, her stride stiff as if it hurt to move.

He followed her, and when he stepped into the other

room she was at the sink, both hands gripping the edge, her head bent.

She looked so lost. So broken... He couldn't help but wrap his arms around her waist and pull her back against him. She didn't fight him, didn't go rigid in his embrace—which worried him to no end—just kept her head down. Her fingers wrapped around the sink's edge.

"I take it things didn't go well at your mom's?" he asked, keeping his voice whisper soft.

Her short, humorless laugh about killed him. "You could say that." She exhaled heavily, her breath washing over his hands. "I'm okay. Just seeing the living room that way..." She lifted her head, bumping his chin. "My mom...when she gets bad...she'll take everything out of cupboards. Desks. Closets. You name it. Until there's no more room for one more knickknack or ceramic figurine or old piece of junk mail anywhere. I'd come home from school and walk into chaos." She twisted and he loosened his hold enough to let her turn in his arms. "And I guess seeing that mess in my own home sort of threw me."

Keeping one hand on her waist, he lightly combed his fingertips through the hair above her ear. "That's my fault. I meant to have the girls clean up before you got back, but they wanted to watch a movie first. Next thing I knew, Abby was asleep. Then Payton."

"They weren't the only ones."

"I shut my eyes for a moment, I swear. And that was

only to block out the nightmare that is *High School Musical*."

As he'd hoped, she smiled. A soft, sad smile that made his heart catch. Their eyes locked. His body stirred. And then she blinked and the spell was broken.

"I've been known to doze off during kid movies, too," she said, collecting herself. She pulled her shoulders back, edged to the side out of his embrace and, cocking a hip, leaned against the table. "They're better than a tranquilizer."

Disappointment coursed through him. Not that he wanted her to be upset—he just wanted her to trust him. To turn to him.

Stupid, really. He wasn't the type of guy women went to for comfort. He was the guy women hooked up with when they wanted a good time, free of entanglements. Free of any of that emotional bullshit that clouded people's judgment.

The way it was clouding his right now. Making him wish for things that would only cause complications. Things he'd never before wanted in his life.

"Sorry about the mess," he said, "I'll just go in and clean—"

"Don't worry about it. The girls and I can take care of it in the morning. I shouldn't have gotten so worked up." She grimaced slightly. "No sense giving my mother more power over me than she already has, right?"

He didn't know what she wanted from him. To agree? She sure as hell didn't want his sympathy. Probably mistook it for pity. "I guess I'll be going, then."

"Oh. Sure. I mean, you must have things to do."

"No. But it is getting late." And since when did he think 10:00 p.m. was late? Life in Jewell was taking its toll on him.

"I'm sorry. I meant to be home sooner," she said so quickly, the words all rushed together. "I left Mom's a while ago but I needed some time to decompress before coming home so I drove around."

"You don't have to apologize to me, Connie," he said wishing he wasn't so out of his element here. With her. "The girls and I were fine." He paused. Frowned. "We had fun," he admitted, surprising himself to realize it was true. Not that he wanted to spend every Friday night playing board games and watching preteen movies, he assured himself. But for one night, a few hours out of the ordinary, it was fine. "They're great kids."

Now she smiled for real. "Yeah. They are." She straightened. "Let me walk you out."

"I think I can find my way. You sure you don't want me to stick around? The least I can do after leaving you with that mess is carry the girls up to bed."

She looked so shocked by his offer he almost took it back. "I'll manage. But…thanks. And thanks again for staying with them."

"No problem." He stuck his hands in his pockets. Took them out again. "So. I guess I'll see you Monday at work."

Her mouth trembled, but then she firmed it. "I guess you will."

He nodded. "Good night."

"Night."

He made it as far as the doorway.

Cursing himself the entire way, he stalked back to her. Ignoring her startled look, he stopped inches from her. "Come here," he said gruffly, holding his arms open.

She stared at him. A sob escaped her and, looking horrified, she covered her mouth with her hand. Her eyes welled. And right before he could pull her into his arms, she leaped at him, wrapped her arms around his neck and clung to him as if she never wanted to let go.

Feeling useless to stop her pain, he shut his eyes and pressed a kiss to the top of her head. "It's okay," he said, having no idea if that was the truth or not. "It'll be okay."

She leaned back to meet his eyes. While hers glistened with tears, she didn't let them fall. "I…I told my mom I was through with her." Her voice was hoarse, as if it hurt just to say the words. "I just can't do it anymore. I tried. I tried so hard to make her happy, to make her be…okay. But she's not. And she's never going to be… normal."

"That's not your fault." He pulled out a chair and tugged her onto his lap. His heart stuttered when she curled into him, her head leaning on his shoulder, her nose pressed against the side of his neck. "It's not up to you to make her okay. Only she can do that."

"I know. It's just…when I was driving around, I realized that all these years I was patting myself on the back, feeling so righteous that I stood by her no matter what. How I took whatever she dished out. I believed that someday I was going to get through to her. I was going to fix her. I was going to help her get better."

He traced light circles over her back. "There's nothing wrong with any of that. What daughter wouldn't want their mother to be healthy in mind and body?"

She played with the edge of his T-shirt sleeve, rubbing the material between her fingers. "I did want all those things," she whispered. "I wanted to have a normal mother. One who didn't suffer from delusions and selfishness. One who wasn't mentally ill. But I didn't want that for her. I wanted it for myself. Because I'm just so tired, so very tired of dealing with her."

The guilt in her voice ripped him apart. "Hey, you're only human. Anyone in your shoes would feel the same way. Anyone else would've given up on her a long time ago." He settled his chin on the top of her head. "You did the best you could for her."

She was silent for so long he wasn't sure she believed him, but then she sighed. "I'm so afraid," she admitted.

His arms tightened around her. "Of what?"

She swallowed audibly. "That I'll somehow end up like her. That the chaos in her mind…the imbalance that makes her the way she is…" She exhaled a shaky breath. "I'm afraid that's in my head, too."

And she broke down, her slight body racked with sobs, her face pressed against his neck. The sound of her tears, of her heartache, burned a hole in his gut. Made him want to punch something. To fix everything for her.

To promise her that there was nothing of her mother in her. To tell her she was a wonderful mother. That she was strong and beautiful and more capable than she gave herself credit for.

He wanted her to know what he saw when he looked at her. She was...amazing.

But he couldn't say any of that. Wouldn't know how to find the words even if he wanted to.

Instead, he tucked her head under his chin and held her close while she cried. And though he felt inadequate, completely out of his element, there was nowhere he'd rather be in that moment than in her kitchen with her in his arms.

CONNIE STARED UP THE STAIRS that led to what used to be J.C.'s apartment and licked her suddenly dry lips. Shifting the potted African violet from one hand to the other, she started to climb.

There was no need to be nervous. This was just a friendly visit. To welcome Matt to his new apartment. With J.C. and Brady recently settled into their new house over on Bradford Street, Matt had moved into the place above J.C.'s grandmother's garage. It was a perfect arrangement. One that gave J.C.'s grandmother a new tenant and Matt a bit of space from the Diamond Dust.

More importantly, it gave him some space from his family.

At the top of the stairs, a country song filtered through the door. She pounded on the wood to be heard.

After he'd left her house, she'd spent the rest of the night tossing and turning. Thinking of what he had given up to save the winery. How he'd stepped in and helped her out with her kids.

How he'd held her while she cried.

No, she hadn't been able to stop thinking about him. So there she was, standing outside his door on a Saturday evening, her pride in her hands. She just hoped, when it was all said and done, that pride wasn't torn into tatters.

The door opened. Matt blinked down at her, looking all sexy and rumpled in a pair of faded jeans and a frayed black sweatshirt. Instead of pulling his hair back, he'd tied a folded dark blue bandanna across his forehead. "Hey," he said, obviously surprised to see her on his new doorstep. "What's up?"

That wasn't quite the enthusiastic welcome she'd been hoping for. Still, she forced a smile. "Hi. Your mom mentioned you were moving in today so I thought I'd stop by. See if I could give you a hand."

One arm holding the top of the door, he leaned against it. The edge of his shirt lifted, giving her a glimpse of skin. "Actually, I'm just finishing up. But thanks."

"Oh. Okay." They'd both helped with J.C. and Brady's move during the week and it must've been a bit too much family time for him since he'd declined any and all offers to help him get settled into the apartment.

The breeze ruffled her hair and she shivered. "Well, anyway," she said, "the girls wanted me to give you this." She lifted the plant. "Happy housewarming."

"You brought me a flower?" he asked, making no move to take it from her.

Jeez, he sounded as if she'd handed him a screaming baby and told him he was the father. Using all of her willpower to ensure she didn't shove the stupid gift into his stomach, she forced a smile.

"Like I said, the girls picked it out. Although their first choice for you was a puppy."

"I'll be lucky to keep this thing alive," he said as he straightened and took the plant. "Please don't give me anything that I'd actually feel guilty about killing."

"So don't kill it," she said in exasperation. "Set it in a sunny window and water it once in a while. Honestly. What is your problem?"

"Nothing. I just…" Looking as serious as she'd ever seen him, he met her eyes. "I'm not cut out to be responsible for something like this. Something that relies on me, that's counting on me."

He wasn't just talking about the flower anymore. And how sad was it that he felt that way about himself? That he didn't, couldn't, see himself the way she saw him. "It's a plant, Matt," she said softly, "not a lifelong commitment."

Smiling, he shook his head. "Right. Thanks." He seemed nervous. Unsure. It was so unlike him, her own nerves returned with a vengeance. Maybe this was a bad idea. Maybe she had the situation between them all wrong.

Maybe he didn't want her anymore.

"Well," she said, her voice so overly bright she winced. "I guess I'll leave you to your evening."

"Do you want to come in?" he asked, sounding as if he hoped she'd say no.

No such luck, buddy. "Sure."

Stepping inside, she tested them both by ever-so-subtly brushing against him. His expression didn't change but she caught the heat that entered his eyes. Heard the slight catch of his breath.

And her own nerves settled. Turned to anticipation.

As he shut the door, she did a slow circle in the middle of the living room. There was a couch and end table underneath the window and a large, flat-screen TV against the wall. No knickknacks. No pictures. No other furniture.

"Can I get you a drink?" he asked. "I have a bottle of Cabernet Sauvignon I think you'd like."

She raised her eyebrows. "The Diamond Dust doesn't make a Cabernet Sauvignon. Is it one of yours?"

He nodded. "From one of the wineries I worked for in Napa."

"I'd love to try it." Though she'd heard about the fabulous wines he'd worked on, she didn't often have a chance to taste them for herself.

He gestured for her to follow him into the tiny kitchen. There were no table or chairs and the counters were bare except for a full wine rack, a can opener and a bottle of dish soap by the sink.

"Where are the girls?" he asked as he pulled a cork-screw from a drawer.

A drawer that held only the corkscrew. Because she wasn't sure of what she'd seen, she pulled it open again. Empty. "Uh…they're with the Pattersons. They have daughters the same age as Payton and Abby so they all play together. They're actually, uh, spending the night."

He opened one of the upper cabinets. She caught a glimpse of several wineglasses, a cereal bowl and two mismatched coffee mugs. "Jeremy Patterson?" he asked, pulling two of the wineglasses down.

"Yeah. Jeremy and his wife, Jennifer," she said, peering past his shoulder into the almost empty cupboard. "You know them?"

He smiled as he poured the wine. "I went to school with Jeremy. Hard to believe he has kids that old."

Connie made a noncommittal sound. Trying to act as casual as possible, she slid open a middle drawer far enough to see it was empty. Forgetting all about casual, she opened the bottom drawer. Then the cabinet next to them. And the next one. Empty. Empty and empty. Ignoring the glass he held out to her, she checked his fridge then the upper cabinets.

Matt leaned back against the counter. "Do I even want to ask what you're looking for?"

"I'm looking for…kitchen stuff. Dishes. Pots. Pans. A box of cereal. I thought you said you were unpacked."

"I am." He swirled his wine in the glass. "I tend to travel light. Usually the wineries I work for provide furnished living space." He took a sip of wine. "I've never had to worry about bringing more than my clothes."

Light? Try nonexistent. "My God, you really are a gypsy, aren't you?"

And yet she'd let him stay with her girls last night, risked the chance of them becoming even more attached to him, knowing he wasn't the type of man to stick around. One who wanted very little to do with his own family, let alone anyone else's.

She picked up her wine, stared at the dark liquid as she swirled it. Glancing up, she caught him watching her with a hunger that caused her stomach to pitch pleasantly. Her blood to heat.

Was it just her own wishful thinking telling her he was more than he seemed? More than she'd ever thought he was.

"How about I get cleaned up?" he asked. "We can go out, get something to eat."

"I don't want to go out," she blurted, then took a long gulp of wine. Maybe at another time, when her stomach wasn't tied in knots, she'd be able to appreciate the complexity of it. "I mean…we could always order in. Eat here."

"I don't think that's a good idea," he said quietly.

Taking her courage in hand, she closed the distance between them. He didn't move but she felt the tension emanating from him. Saw it in the tightness of his jaw. His hooded eyes.

"What's the matter? Are you afraid to be alone with me now that the girls aren't around to chaperone?" Though she'd been teasing, he seared her with a heated look and her jaw dropped. Her mouth went dry as the realization shook her. "That's it, isn't it?" Feminine power surged through her. Gave her the confidence to press against him. "Afraid you won't be able to control yourself?" she asked on a breathless whisper.

"That's it," he said, plucking her wine from her hand. "You're cut off." As she stood there with her mouth gaping open, he edged to the side. Set her glass by the sink. "I hadn't realized you were such a lightweight." He finished his wine in one long drink then cleared his throat. "Now, how about we get some dinner?"

Doubts, about herself, about him, crept into her mind. Had her face heating. Made her rethink her purpose for being there. But then she glanced at Matt. Saw that same unguarded look she'd seen in his eyes several times before. A longing. A warmth that convinced her he felt something for her.

Even if he didn't know it yet.

But she knew it. Believed it. Knew she could trust it. That she could trust herself and her instincts when it came to him. Most of all, she trusted him.

"I don't want any dinner," she told him, feeling more vulnerable standing before him than she'd ever felt in her life. More exposed than if she'd been naked on Main Street. "And I didn't really come here to help you unpack or organize your cupboards. I came here—" she rushed on when he opened his mouth to speak "—because I want to be with you."

CHAPTER FIFTEEN

MATT DIDN'T MOVE. COULD barely breathe.

She was killing him.

"I think I blacked out there for a moment," he said gruffly. "Would you mind repeating that?"

She rolled her eyes but he noticed she'd twisted her fingers together at her waist. "I want to be with you."

He exhaled heavily. "Yeah. That's what I thought you said." It was like a dream come true. So why wasn't he kissing her already? "Why?"

She blinked. "Excuse me?"

"Why do you want to be with me? Why now, I mean. Last week you made it perfectly clear you had no desire to sleep with me."

She stared at him as if he'd recently suffered a blow to the head. "You want me to give you reasons? Now?"

Hell, no. What he wanted was to take her in his arms. To touch her. Make love to her until both of them were so completely satiated they couldn't think straight. Until the reasons didn't matter.

Because he cared about her, too. He felt things for her he'd never experienced before. Desire, yes, that was familiar and something he could handle. But it was more than that. She invaded his thoughts when he didn't want to think about her. Warmed his heart when he needed to stay detached. Made him start to think that maybe the life he'd also been afraid of—a life with a family, with people who counted on you—wouldn't be so bad after all.

But they did matter. She mattered. For the first time in his life someone meant more to him than his own wants and needs.

"I want to know why you want to be with me," he said. "Is it because of last night?"

Last night when he'd held her in his arms while she'd cried, his heart breaking for her.

"Yes," she said dryly, crossing her arms, her mouth set, "this is because of last night. I'm just so darn grateful to you for watching my kids and buying them pizza and holding me while I fell apart that, well, I thought I should do something for you in return. And sending you a candygram just didn't seem like it would cut it."

He nodded. Needing something to do with his hands so he wouldn't reach for her, he picked up her still-full wineglass and took a sip. "Okay. So it's not gratitude."

"I'm attracted to you," she blurted, tossing her hands in the air. "And I...I care about you. But if you're not interested in me, just say so."

I care about you.

Such a generic statement. And yet it scared the crap out of him. He set the glass down and advanced on her slowly. She backed up a step then stood her ground. He almost smiled. Connie always stood her ground.

"Oh, I'm interested," he told her softly. "I haven't

been able to stop thinking of you, to stop wanting you. I'm not used to waiting so long for something I want."

She lifted her chin, but her eyes were wary. "I'm worth waiting for."

He grinned and set both hands on her slim waist, his thumbs on her hip bones. "I don't doubt that."

"You didn't kiss me." She laid her hands against his chest. His heart kicked up under her palms. "Since that night at the wedding," she continued, her throat working. "I thought maybe you'd changed your mind."

And yet she'd still come to him. Her courage humbled him. "I wanted to change my mind. I didn't want to want you. But I couldn't stop."

"You could've kissed me last night."

He shifted his hands to her tight ass, easing her forward until their hips bumped. "You were hurting. I didn't want to take advantage."

"That's sweet," she said, making him sound like some damn choirboy when that couldn't be further from the truth. "But what if I want you to take advantage? What if I want you to just…take me?"

At her words, his pulse pounded in his ears, his body hardened. "We both know what we're getting into here," he said roughly. "This isn't a mistake."

Her eyes warmed. Her soft hand cupped his cheek. "No. This isn't a mistake."

That was all he needed to hear. He pressed his mouth to hers. He meant to keep the kiss gentle. To seduce her slowly, to show her how good they could be together. To show her with actions what he couldn't tell her with his words. How much she meant to him. How badly he wanted her.

But she jerked, her hands gripping his hair as she opened her mouth under his. With a moan, he slid his tongue between her lips to taste her. She rubbed against him, the feel of her soft, slim body, her small, round breasts inflaming him. He wanted to lift her onto the counter and take her, just as she'd said, right there in the empty kitchen.

But this was Connie. She deserved better than a quick, rough coupling. She deserved...everything. Everything he had to give her.

Still kissing her, he lifted her from beneath her rear. She clung to him, wrapping those long, firm legs around his waist as he carried her through the living room to the bedroom he'd yet to sleep in.

Reaching along the wall, he finally managed to find the light switch. "Shit," he muttered, tearing his mouth from hers. "I forgot. I don't have a bed yet."

That's what she did to him. Made him forget everything but her. He'd figured he'd camp out on the couch for a few nights until he had time to get to the furniture store, buy a bed and maybe a dresser. For now, the room was completely empty except for his large duffel bag and a closet full of his clothes.

Connie unwound her legs and glanced over her shoulder. "Seems to me you have a perfectly good floor. It'd be a shame to let all that empty space go to waste."

Unable to stop touching her, he skimmed his hands

up her arms and down again. "I've always admired how practical you are."

She smiled and stepped back, out of his reach. "You ain't seen nothing yet."

And then, crossing her arms, she took hold of the bottom of her shirt and stripped it over her head.

His breath clogged in his lungs. His arousal jumped behind his zipper. "You're so damn beautiful," he said, not caring that his tone was reverent or that he'd never before had a woman affect him, body and soul, the way Connie did standing there in a plain white bra. A faint blush stained her cheeks but her eyes met his. Remained on his even as she reached behind her, unhooked the bra and slid it down her arms.

She was small, her breasts firm, their pink tips tightening under his gaze. She was everything he wanted. Fisting one hand in her hair, he tugged her head back. Her eyes widened. Her hands clutched his shoulders, her short nails digging into his skin. Wrapping his other arm around her waist, he bent her back, holding her there so he could feast on her.

He took one breast into his mouth, used his lips and tongue, his teeth slightly scraping over her nipples until she was panting. Until she squirmed in his arms, her skin heated. The sounds she made, soft gasps of delight, raw moans of pleasure, ripped through him, shredded the thin hold he had on his control.

She clawed at his shirt and he yanked her upright, let go long enough to tug off his shirt and the bandanna on his head. Tossed them aside. Then he kissed her again. Her hands raced over him, over his shoulders, down his

arms, across his chest, as if she couldn't get enough of
him. Her nails raked his scalp lightly as she combed her
fingers through his hair, brushed her fingertips down
the side of his face, along the edge of his jaw.

She drove him crazy. Need grew until he couldn't
stop himself from dragging her to the floor. Frantic for
her, he unhooked her jeans, pulled down the zipper. She
lifted her hips and shoved the material down her thighs.
He stood long enough to rid himself of his own jeans
and grab a condom from his wallet before joining her
on the floor again. Careful to keep his weight on his
elbows, he settled on top of her.

He meant to slow down, take his time, to touch and
taste her, every inch of her, but she kissed him hungrily,
her soft, warm hands sliding over his body. She wrapped
one long leg around his waist, her foot rubbing the back
of his calf. She was all subtle curves and silky, sweet-
smelling skin. He stroked her, from her shoulder down
over the roundness of her breast to the flat planes of her
stomach. He brushed his fingers against her tight curls
and she lifted her hips. Sliding one finger over her, he
found her hot and wet and ready for him.

And he couldn't wait another moment to make her
his.

Without taking the time to wonder about the pos-
sessive thought, he sheathed himself with the condom,
kissed her deeply and slid inside her.

CONNIE MOANED INTO MATT'S mouth as he filled her.
Stretched her. Inch by slow, glorious inch until they

THE PRODIGAL SON

were completely joined. He paused, whether to give her time to adjust to his size, his hardness or to gain a bit of control for himself, she wasn't sure. He lay on top of her, stealing her breath. He was hot. Hard. Pulsing inside of her.

Finally, he lifted his head. "Okay?" he asked tightly.

Okay? She was aroused to the point of aching. Her heart was racing, her blood flowed thick and heavy through her veins. She was so much more than okay. She was wonderful.

And he was on top of her, his hard, hot body pressing her into the rough carpet. His jaw tight. His eyes as serious as she'd ever seen him.

Instead of answering, she held his gaze captive and then rocked against him. His breath hissed out. His arms, close to her head, began to shake. Feminine power—the knowledge that she could make this man, this sexy, self-confident man, tremble with need—flowed through her. Holding his wonderful, handsome face in her hands, she met his thrust again. And again.

With a low growl, he bent and kissed her fiercely as he gripped her hips and thrust into her. Sensations poured through her. Sweat coated their skin. The air filled with the sounds of their bodies moving together, their harsh breathing. Her whimpers of pleasure.

He slid his hands underneath her, tipped her hips up and plunged into her, over and over, harder and harder. Needing something to ground her, she held on to his arms. His skin was slick under her fingers. His muscles tense.

But it was his face that mesmerized her. His familiar, handsome face was set in harsh lines. The green eyes she'd looked into a hundred, a thousand times before were now serious, intense. Searching hers for something…something she wasn't sure she could give him. Something she was afraid to give him.

Letting go of her, he took both her hands in his, linked his fingers through hers and stretched her arms over her head. Pinned her hands to the carpet. She arched against him. Her heart stuttered. It was hard to breathe. Her climax was there, just right there, out of her reach. And still he drove into her, working her until she moved under him like a piston. Her breath came out in ragged gasps.

And then, as if he knew what he was doing to her, as if he knew how he made her feel, Matt smiled. A sexy smile that was so warm and a bit cocky and so totally Matt…. She tumbled over the edge.

Her vision blurred. Pleasure spiked, sped through her, leaving her gasping, her muscles quivering, her limbs weak as she cried out. Two more pumps and Matt bowed back as he groaned with his own climax.

He collapsed on top of her, his body sticky with sweat, his heart racing furiously against her chest, his face pressed to the side of her neck. His weight on her pushed the breath from her lungs. She gulped in air, stroked her fingers through his silky hair. Gradually she became aware that her back and butt were sore from the carpet.

"You were right," he mumbled, his lips moving against her skin. "You were definitely worth the wait."

Her heart swelled and she kissed his temple.

Take me, she'd told him.

She'd wanted him to love her. To give her pleasure. And he had. Completely. Thoroughly.

But he hadn't just taken her body. He'd taken a piece of her heart, too.

MATT AWOKE A FEW HOURS later, his body stiff and sore, his bare feet freezing, his knees stinging from rug burn.

He grinned. He couldn't remember when he'd felt better.

Shoving his hair out of his eyes with one hand he reached out with the other, only to encounter the empty floor. He jackknifed up into a sitting position. Sunlight streamed through the window, and in the pale yellow glow Connie stood, her back to him, her hips wiggling as she pulled her jeans up and fastened them.

"Going somewhere?" he asked softly.

In only her bra and those snug jeans, she whirled around in surprise, her lips parted.

His body tightened. Heated. She was like some sexy fairy come to life with her short, messy hair, pale lips and dark eyes. He'd left his mark on her, he thought, his gaze lingering above the cup of her bra where his stubble had scratched her delicate skin. Possessiveness unlike any he'd ever felt, ever wanted to feel, swelled inside him at the sight of that pink mark marring the perfection of her pale, creamy skin. Under his scrutiny, her nipples beaded, pressed against the thin material of her bra.

He pushed back to a sitting position and held out his hand. "Come here." His voice was gruff as want and need collided inside him.

She stepped forward then shook her head, smiling ruefully. "I'd like to, believe me. There's nothing I'd like better—well, except for maybe that bed I insisted we didn't need."

Finding her shirt on the floor, she shook out the wrinkles, turned it right-side-out and tugged it on.

"Now don't do that." He got to his feet, wrapped the blanket he'd found last night to keep them warm as they'd slept—and made love one more time—on the floor. "I promise... I'll buy a bed. The biggest, softest bed you've ever slept in. In the meantime, if you're tired of the floor, we could always try the couch." With one hand holding the blanket, he used the other hand to comb through her hair then cupped the back of her head. "Or we could see if there's room for two in the shower."

Take me, she'd told him last night, blowing his mind and his world apart.

There were at least a dozen places right in this tiny apartment he'd like to take her. And he hadn't given up on that kitchen counter fantasy.

"I don't want you to go," he admitted before pressing his mouth to hers. She responded immediately, her lips warming, softening under his. But when he went to deepen the kiss, to pull her closer, she laughed and stepped back.

"I have to," she said, stroking his ego by sounding as disappointed as he felt. "I have to pick the girls up in fifteen minutes."

Right. The girls.

He slowly removed his hand from the silk of her hair. Curled it around a fistful of blanket and forced a smile. "Next time we'll check out the shower's size."

She gave him a puzzled look. "Yeah. Sure." She hesitated, chewed on her lower lip. He could almost see her brain working, could sense her nerves. "You know, I could come back," she said in a rush. "With the girls, I mean. We usually make a big breakfast on Sundays—pancakes, home fries...that sort of thing...."

Cold washed over him, prickled his skin. Have her girls here, in his new space, bringing with them their clutter and bright smiles and constant questions? He could so easily picture it, see them all together either here or at Connie's place. The perfect scene. The perfect family.

Except one thing didn't belong. Him.

But when he spoke, he made sure none of the alarm racing through his blood could be detected in his voice. "That'd be great," he lied, "but I don't have any groceries."

"We could pick some up," she said as he turned his back to her and pulled on his jeans, too desperate to get dressed to bother with his underwear first.

"Actually, since you're heading out, I should probably

do some shopping." He faced her, crossed his arms over his bare chest. "I wanted to drive over to Danville anyway. See what furniture shops are there."

"Oh. Okay. Well, how about you come for dinner when you get back? We could—"

"No."

She flinched. Damn it. He hadn't meant to say that quite so vehemently. He just didn't want her to get the wrong idea. About him. About them.

"Sorry," he said, pulling on his ear. "I just…I don't know when I'll be back. From Danville. Why don't we just…talk…tomorrow at work?"

"Sure," she said slowly, the clear hurt in her eyes making his chest feel tight. "I guess I'll see you tomorrow then."

And she bolted out of the room as if she couldn't wait another second to get away from him.

He shoved a hand through his hair.

Shit.

He caught up with her as she was opening the front door. Slipping between her and the exit, he shut the door again and stood in front of it. "Look, I didn't make myself very clear—"

"Believe me, you were perfectly clear. You want to have sex with me, when it's convenient for you, of course—"

"Hey, now," he said, bristling, "you came to me, remember?" He hadn't used her. Hadn't treated her with anything less than the utmost respect.

"It's not something I'll soon forget," she said icily,

closing the distance between them to poke his chest with her finger. "And the only reason I came over was because I…" She pressed her lips together as if taking the time to gather her thoughts, her emotions. "I thought that underneath that charming persona you hide behind was a man I could trust enough to share my body with. Maybe even share my feelings with. God, I…I thought I could even let you be a part of my children's lives." She shook her head. "Pretty stupid, huh? Because you don't want any of that. You'd much rather keep everyone who cares about you at arm's length."

He stood perfectly still, afraid if he so much as blinked, all the clashing emotions inside him would burst free. "You're blowing this way out of proportion. Of course you can trust me."

"Can I trust you with my daughters' feelings? With my own?"

"I would never do anything to purposely hurt you or the girls." Didn't she see that's why he wanted to keep his distance from them?

"No, I know you wouldn't," she said quietly. "But that's not enough. I want someone in my life who isn't careless with us. Who understands that while our life may be scheduled and ordinary, it's also filled with un-expected moments—both big and small—that make it all the more wonderful. Who sees that being part of a family, that relying on others and having them care for you doesn't make them weak. It makes them stronger."

She tried to brush past him and panic set in, had him

shifting to block her. He couldn't let her go. "Let's talk this through. We can work this out—"

"We could. I'm sure we could figure out a way for you to keep your independence, for us to have a casual relationship, one with no strings and no messy emotions involved. But I want those strings," she said emphatically, her eyes bright with unshed tears, "and those emotions, no matter how messy they may be. I want…for once in my life…someone to put me first." Her voice cracked and it took all he had not to reach for her. "I think I deserve at least that much."

Because she was fighting tears, and her body was trembling, he didn't have any other choice but to step aside and let her go. Leaning one arm on the door frame above his head, he watched her race down the stairs and climb into her car. She had responsibilities to get back to. Daughters to raise. People who counted on her.

And though he was stuck in Jewell, he still had the one thing he'd always craved. He needed to hold on to the one thing he'd fought for his entire life. His freedom.

So why did it feel as if he'd lost something even more precious?

CHAPTER SIXTEEN

"THIS IS AN UNUSUAL PLACE for a mother-son bonding session," Matt said as he approached his mother later that afternoon. The sun hid behind dark gray clouds, and the cold air bit through his jacket.

"That's true." Kneeling on the ground, Diane brushed dirt off his father's headstone with one gloved hand. "But in this case, it's an appropriate spot."

Matt shoved his own hands into his pockets as his mother tidied the grave. He hadn't been to the Oakdale Cemetery since his father's funeral...sure as hell wouldn't be here now if his mother hadn't called him an hour ago and insisted.

He studied the simplicity of his father's headstone. It was a deep caramel color with subtle flecks of mahogany and bronze, the top and sides gently curved. His father's name, the dates of his birth and his death and the line Lost for now, but loved forever, were scrolled on the right.

His father's life reduced to three lines etched in stone.

His mom leaned back and wiped the dirt off her pants. As she straightened, Matt helped her get to her feet. They stood in silence, his mother's head bowed.

But Matt wasn't sure what he'd ask for if he prayed, so he didn't. His father was dead and no amount of wishing could bring him back.

Nothing could change everything that had happened between them.

"You remind me of him," Diane said, lifting her head. "In so many ways."

Matt bristled. "I'm nothing like him."

"You have his eyes. His stubbornness." She smiled. "Your love for the land, your strong work ethic, how you enjoy nothing more than tackling a problem or new adventure…even the way you hold your head. Those all come from your father."

He kept his mouth shut.

"He loved you."

He remembered what Connie had said about his dad the night of the stag party. *He followed your career. Used to brag to me about you. He was proud of you.*

Matt slowly shook his head. "I was a disappointment to him."

"No," his mother said, stepping in front of him so he was forced to meet her eyes. "That's not true. He was disappointed you didn't want the same things he did, but he was never disappointed in you. He just…he made mistakes with you. So many. But he was too stubborn, and when he finally realized he needed to fix those mistakes, it was too late."

"He never asked me to come back."

She looked over her shoulder at the grave. "I think he

was scared you'd reject any overture he made. And part of him still hoped you'd come back on your own."

He fisted his hands in his pockets. "When I didn't, you decided to take matters into your own hands, is that it?"

"I decided to do whatever it took to bring you home. And even though you might hold on to your anger at me for as long as you've been angry with your father, I'd do it again."

"Because you did what Dad wanted."

She huffed out an exasperated breath. "Because the Diamond Dust is where you belong."

Was it? He didn't used to believe it, but working alongside his brothers hadn't been as bad as he'd thought it would be. And he'd never wanted a small-town life. Too scheduled and settled. It was exactly what he'd spent half his life running away from.

It was the kind of life he'd have with Connie and the girls… Why did that make it sound more appealing?

"What do you want me to say, Mom?" he asked wearily. "That I'm glad you handled things the way you did? I forgive you? That's not going to happen. Not today anyway."

"I know. Besides, I'm not the one you need to forgive." She linked her arm with his, then nodded at his father's grave. "He is."

"YOU WANTED TO SEE ME?" Connie asked Aidan early Monday morning as she stood in his office doorway.

"Yes." He waved her in. "Have a seat."

She glanced around the room first, no one in either of the arm chairs across from Aidan, no long, lean body stretched out on the sofa. Matt wasn't here.

Good.

She stepped inside. She still hadn't figured out how she was going to avoid him at work. Yesterday she'd been too busy trying not to break down, trying not to let her girls see her heartache to worry about what could possibly happen come Monday morning.

And now that Monday was here? She was scared out of her mind that she was going to come face-to-face with him. That one look into his green eyes and she'd throw her pride and her principles to the wind.

Or worse. Admit to him exactly how she felt about him.

From behind his desk, Aidan leaned forward and lowered his reading glasses as if to get a better look at her. "You okay?"

God, she must look even worse than she felt. And she felt pretty damn crappy. Her entire body ached, and her eyes were gritty and red-rimmed from lack of sleep. "I'm fine."

He studied her as she sat on the edge of one of the chairs. She kept her gaze on the shelves of books behind him. So what if he didn't believe her? It wasn't as if her job depended on her looking good. Or being 100 percent truthful.

He sat back, took his glasses off and set them on the desk in front of him. "We're going ahead with your idea."

"Great. What idea is that?"

"Holding special events at the Diamond Dust," he said, speaking to her as if she'd forgotten to bring her wits along with her to this meeting, "with a focus on weddings. And we want you to be in charge."

A soft buzzing filled her head. "Excuse me?"

"It was your idea, so you should take the lead. We'll discuss your salary after you've come up with a list of what you figure your responsibilities will be. I'm assuming you can have something to me by…say… Wednesday?"

It took her a moment to realize she was nodding. "Wait. If I'm doing that, what about the vineyards?"

"Matt's more than capable of handling them."

And just like that, the buzzing increased, shifting from a couple of bees to a couple dozen chain saws. This was what she'd wanted, she reminded herself. Now, not only would she be able to help the Diamond Dust grow, she'd also have her own position within the company. She'd have security.

No longer would she have to worry about where she belonged.

"But…I thought you and Matt were against hosting events here."

"We discussed it over dinner last night at Mom's—"

"Matt had Sunday dinner at your mom's?" she asked, unable to keep the shock from her voice.

"It surprised us, too. Especially when he gave a business presentation during dessert. He convinced me hosting events won't hurt the Diamond Dust's reputation or affect the wine we make, especially if we have separate positions for both, instead of trying to divide someone's attention between the winemaking and the event planning."

"And you want me in charge of making this new venture work?"

"We do."

It was exactly what she'd dreamed would happen when she'd approached Aidan and his brothers with the idea. She'd been so desperate to carve out her own niche at the winery, to ensure she'd always be needed there, wanted there, that she'd been willing to give up her vineyards, the work she loved, to make that happen.

Matt had ridden to her rescue. He'd convinced Aidan to go along with her idea despite his own feelings about hosting special events at the winery. He'd put her first.

Because he felt guilty over pushing her aside as vineyard manager? About how things had ended between them? She swallowed in an attempt to dislodge the lump that formed in her throat. Or had he done it because he cared about her? Because he wanted her to be happy. She didn't know. Couldn't spend any more time wondering about it, either, or she'd drive herself mad.

All she knew was what she had to do next.

"Thank you for the offer," she said, her voice unsteady. "But I can't accept it."

"I know you probably don't want to leave the vineyards—"

"You're right. I don't. But that's not why I can't accept the position. It's because...I quit."

His expression dour, he picked up his reading glasses and swung them back and forth. "That's not funny."

She stood. Because her hands were shaking, she clasped them together behind her back. "I'm not joking."

Aidan slowly set his glasses back down again. "You can't quit."

"I can and I am," she said, her throat so tight she had to push the words out. "I'm sorry, but I can't give you two weeks' notice. I'll be leaving today." She had to get away from there as soon as possible. Or she might change her mind.

"The hell you will." His eyes flashed, his mouth formed a grim line. "You can't just quit. The Diamond Dust needs you. I need you."

Her heart lurched. "You don't know, you couldn't possibly know how much that means to me to hear you say that. But...I can't stay here. I can't be a part of the Diamond Dust."

His eyes narrowed. "Is this because of something Matt did?"

She shook her head. "Ever since your dad first hired me, all I ever wanted was to be a part of the Diamond Dust. A real part." She laughed softly, but the sound held no humor. "I used to dream that one day, you and I would run the winery together, as full partners. I had it all planned out. God, I even wrote up a business proposal about it. Made a list of the reasons you should take me on as a partner, a financial sheet outlining how I would invest in the business. That's what I came up here to talk to you about that day you told me you were going into partnership with your brothers."

He rubbed his forehead. "Does Mom know about any of this?"

"No. And don't tell her. Please. I...I don't want her to think any of this is her fault."

He dropped his hand. "Isn't it? If not for her black-mailing us into going into business together—"

"She did what she thought she had to do. And who knows? Maybe this really will be for the best for you all." Her lip quivered and she firmed it. "I just...you have to know how much you mean to me. How much working at the Diamond Dust has meant to me."

"Don't go," he said quietly. "We can work something out."

"I can't. I can't be faced with something I want so badly, something I know I'll never have," she said, not caring if he knew she was talking about way more than just her job. "It's not fair and I won't do that to myself. Not anymore."

MATT ADDED A BOTTLE OF Merlot to the shipping box. He wasn't hiding—no matter what his conscience said. He was in one of the back rooms of the gift shop with Kathleen and Janice boxing up shipments to be sent to wine club members, because they needed an extra pair of hands. Not because he was trying to avoid running into Connie.

He wondered if he could just hang out in that back room for the next year or so. Until he was free to leave the Diamond Dust. And when he did go, he was going to make sure it was for good.

"What the hell did you do to Connie?"

They all looked over at the door to see Aidan glowering at Matt. Kathleen and Janice exchanged a questioning glance. Matt slapped the flaps on the top of the box closed. "Can one of you tape this up for me?" he asked, not even looking at the women. He stalked over to Aidan. Jerked his head toward the hallway. "Back here."

It was then that he saw Brady behind Aidan, his face, as usual, calm and composed. They walked down the hall single file, Matt in the lead. He pushed open the glass door that led to the large, covered patio that ran the width of the building. Despite the driving rain hitting the patio roof, he went outside.

He waited until his brothers had joined him before demanding, "Did you see Connie today? Is she all right?"

Brady shook his head. "You've got it bad, don't you?"

The back of his neck heated and he welcomed the breeze that flowed over him, peppering his skin with rain. "I was just wondering if Aidan talked to her about being in charge of events here. That's all."

Aidan stood by the door. Probably to avoid getting his hair wet. "I offered Connie the position."

Matt's heart seemed to stop beating. "And?"

Aidan just shrugged. "What's really going on between you and Connie?" he asked, watching him carefully.

"Don't go there," Brady murmured at the same time as Matt snapped, "Nothing."

Which was the truth. After they'd made love—twice—after she'd spent the night in his arms, she'd walked away from him. Because he couldn't give her what she wanted. Couldn't just tell her what she needed most to hear.

He hadn't been enough for her.

And because of that, he'd lost her.

But that was okay. He'd been crazy to suggest they try to work something out. His thoughts had still been clouded by lust. By his want for her. His hunger to have her again. There were too many risks involved in being in a relationship, any kind of relationship. Someone was always trying to change you. To get you to fit into their mold of who they thought you should be.

Like his father had.

"You slept with her," Aidan said flatly.

Matt's head snapped back. "What am I, wearing a sign?"

Brady clapped him hard on the shoulder. "No. But you just walked into that one."

"He's right." Aidan closed the distance between them. "I was just guessing. What the hell were you thinking, having sex with Connie?"

Matt rubbed the back of his neck. "Do you really want me to answer that?"

"Damn it, Matt. You can't go around sleeping with our employees."

He didn't want to sleep with their employees. Didn't want anyone other than Connie.

Fear gripped him, left him dizzy as he realized just how true that statement was. As he realized just how badly he'd blown it with her. "I'll fix it."

Somehow. Some way.

"How?" Aidan asked. "Are you going to climb into your time machine and make sure it never happened in the first place?"

"I said I'll fix it," he growled. "Now back off."

Aidan regarded him with what Matt could only describe as pity. "It's too late. She's gone."

"What do you mean?" he asked, ignoring the feeling of uneasiness that came over him.

"She didn't accept the new position. She quit the Diamond Dust."

"What? When?"

"Just now before I came over here. Said she was going to clean out her desk and that she'd be gone within the hour."

Matt began to pace, his movements stiff. No. No, no, no. She wasn't supposed to quit. She was supposed to accept the job. He'd figured it all out. Had convinced Aidan it was a good idea to hold special events there because he'd wanted to give Connie something. Wanted her to have her spot at the winery.

He'd wanted to keep her close even if he couldn't be with her.

Instead, all he did was push her even further away.

He had to stop her. He had to get her back.

He didn't realize he was running until he heard his brothers' surprised shouts, their questions as he raced across the yard toward the road. Rain pelted his face, his bare arms. Cold pricked his skin. And still he kept running, his work boots pounding the ground, splashing water up the backs of his legs.

All he could think about, all he cared about, was getting to Connie before it was too late.

THE FRONT DOOR SLAMMED with a resounding bang. Connie jumped and whirled around in her chair just as Matt came storming into her office. Her eyes widened.

"What the hell do you think you're doing?" he asked.

She opened her mouth, only to shut it again. Then looked outside at the still-pouring rain and back to him again. His hair was plastered to his head, the wet strands sticking to his cheeks and the sides of his neck. Water ran in rivulets down his sharply drawn face, dripped off the ends of his hair to soak into his already-saturated shirt. His jeans were wet from his knees down to his work boots.

"Are you all right?" she couldn't help but ask. "Let me get you a towel."

She started past him, figuring he could use a few kitchen towels to mop up some of the water, but he grabbed her arm and tugged her against him.

"I asked what you think you're doing," he said, his voice a low rumble.

Stiffening, she pushed against his wet chest. "I think I'm about to get really mean if you don't let go of me."

Too bad her voice lacked heat. Instead, even to her own ears she sounded unsure. Wary. Her pulse pounded under his hand. She just hoped he didn't notice.

"You can't quit your job," he said, his grip loosening, but not enough for her to get free.

"Funny, that's the same thing Aidan said. So I'll tell you what I told him. I can quit. And I did."

"You love the Diamond Dust."

She did. So much. But this was exactly why she had to leave. She couldn't work there day in and day out, worried she'd run into him. It hurt too much.

"I have loved working here," she admitted, not meeting his eyes. "But it's time for me to move on."

He rubbed his thumb across the sensitive skin of her inner wrist. "Because of me."

At his soft words, she brought her head up. "Is that what this is about? You feel guilty? Because if so, then you can leave."

"Guilty?" he asked, yanking her to her toes. A small gasp escaped her. "Hell, yeah, I feel guilty. And frustrated. And angry. And so confused I can barely see straight."

Her throat went dry. She couldn't do this. Couldn't let him confuse the issue, confuse her feelings. Not when she was already so close to the breaking point.

She tugged her arm, but he held firm. "Please let me go," she whispered, staring at his chest.

His fingers tightened briefly. "I can't."

"Please," she repeated, hating that he'd reduced her to begging. That her voice hitched with emotion. "I...I can't do this right now."

Finally, he slowly peeled his fingers from her wrist. She quickly crossed over to stand behind her desk. Somehow it felt better to have that distance between them. Safer.

Matt stared at her, his expression hard. "You need someone steady, someone reliable in your life."

"Yes," she said slowly, rubbing her wrist where his fingers had branded her. "We've already been through this."

"I can be that man. Let me be that man for you."

She shut her eyes wearily. "I appreciate that you want to try—I really do—but we both know that's not who you are. You were completely freaked out yesterday when I suggested you spend some time with me and the girls. Now you want me to believe that was, what...just a mistake?"

He wiped a hand over his face, pushing his hair off his forehead. "I..." His mouth thinned. "I was scared." He met her eyes. "I don't want to hurt you, Connie. You or the girls."

Though his admission touched her, she couldn't back down. "I know that. And while I also know you may not mean to hurt us, what if you do? What if you decide to take off once your year here is up? How am I going to explain that to my children?"

"I won't," he said, sounding so much like he meant it, she wanted to believe him.

But this was Matt. And she couldn't take that chance with her daughters or with her own heart. "I'm sorry. I can't let you play house with us while you're here, only to watch you walk away when fun time is over."

Her words hung in the air a moment before Matt began stalking toward her, the intensity of his gaze pinning her in place. "Is that what you think?" he asked quietly, dangerously. When he rounded the desk, she snapped out of her haze and took a step back. Then another. But he kept coming, getting closer. "That I think you're some goddamn plaything I can toy with until I lose interest?"

"No, I—"

"I love you," he said roughly, not stopping even when her back was pressed against the wall. "I love you and I want to be with you."

She couldn't stop a sound of shock from rising in her throat. Couldn't help the surge of joy, of hope that rushed through her. "Matt, I—"

"I may not be the kind of guy who sticks around," he continued ruthlessly, his anger so palpable she was surprised steam wasn't rising from his skin. "But when I'm with you, I don't feel like that guy. I don't want to be him. Not anymore."

She trembled. Kept her hands at her sides instead of touching him like she wanted. She had to be sure. "Who do you feel like?"

"I feel like the guy who deserves you." He lifted a hand, lightly traced the arch of her brow, the curve of her cheek with his finger. "I want to be with you, Connie.

You and the girls. I want to see where this leads. Can you…could you give me the chance to be that guy for you?"

"Yes," she whispered, cupping his wonderful handsome face in her hands. "Yes, I can give you that chance. I love you, too."

Pressing his forehead against hers, he swallowed. "Thank you."

Then he kissed her. She clung to him, water seeping through her own shirt as she wrapped her arms around his neck and held on tight. The prodigal son of the Diamond Dust had finally found where he belonged.

✤ ✤ ✤ ✤ ✤

Harlequin Super Romance®

COMING NEXT MONTH

Available June 14, 2011

REQUEST YOUR FREE BOOKS!
2 FREE NOVELS PLUS 2 FREE GIFTS!

Harlequin®

Super Romance®

Exciting, emotional, unexpected!

"THANKS FOR NOT TURNING ON THE LIGHTS," Tyler said. "I'm a mess."

"Not in my book." Even in low light, Alex had a good view of her yellow shirt plastered to her body. It was all he could do not to reach for her, mud and all. But the next move needed to be hers, not his.

She slicked her wet hair back and squeezed some water out of the ends as she glanced upward. "I like the sound of the rain on a tin roof."

"Me, too."

She met his gaze briefly and looked away. "Where's the sink?"

"At the far end, beyond the last stall."

Tyler's running shoes squished as she walked down the aisle between the rows of stalls. She glanced sideways at Alex. "So how much of a cowboy are you these days? Do you ride the range and stuff?"

"I ride." He liked being able to say that. "Why?"

"Just wondered. Last summer, you were still a city boy. You even told me you weren't the cowboy type, but you're...different now."

He wasn't sure if that was a good thing or a bad thing. Maybe she preferred city boys to cowboys. "How am I different?"

"Well, you dress differently, and your hair's a little longer. Your face seems a little more chiseled, but maybe that's because of your hair. Also, there's something else, something harder to define, an attitude…"

"Are you saying I have an attitude?"

"Not in a bad way. It's more like a quiet confidence."

He was flattered, but still he had to laugh. "I just admitted a while ago that I have all kinds of doubts about this event tomorrow. That doesn't seem like quiet confidence to me."

"This isn't about your job, it's about…your…" She took a deep breath. "It's about your sex appeal, okay? I have no business talking about it, because it will only make me want to do things I shouldn't do." She started toward the end of the barn. "Now, where's that sink? We need to get cleaned up and go back to the house. Dinner is probably ready, and I—"

He spun her around and pulled her into his arms, mud and all. "Let's do those things." Then he kissed her, knowing that she would kiss him back, knowing that this time he would take that kiss where he wanted it to go. And she would let him.

Follow Tyler and Alex's wild adventures in
SHOULD'VE BEEN A COWBOY
Available June 2011 only from Harlequin® Blaze™
wherever books are sold.

SPECIAL EDITION

Life, Love and Family

LOVE CAN BE FOUND IN THE MOST UNLIKELY PLACES, ESPECIALLY WHEN YOU'RE NOT LOOKING FOR IT...

Failed marriages, broken families and disappointment. Cecilia and Brandon have both been unlucky in love and life and are ripe for an intervention. Good thing Brandon's mother happens to stumble upon this matchmaking project. But will Brandon be able to open his eyes and get away from his busy career to see that all he needs is right there in front of him?

FIND OUT IN

WHAT THE SINGLE DAD WANTS...

BY *USA TODAY* BESTSELLING AUTHOR

MARIE FERRARELLA

AVAILABLE IN JUNE 2011
WHEREVER BOOKS ARE SOLD.